EXPLORER ACADEMY

THE *STAR DUNES*

TRUDI TRUEIT

UNDER THE *Stars*

FOR JACQUES, WITH LOVE, FROM KIDDO —T.T.

Since 1888, the National Geographic Society has funded more than 12,000 research, exploration, and preservation projects around the world. The Society receives funds from National Geographic Partners, LLC, funded in part by your purchase. A portion of the proceeds from this book supports this vital work. To learn more, visit natgeo.com/info.

NATIONAL GEOGRAPHIC and Yellow Border Design are trademarks of the National Geographic Society, used under license.

Under the Stars is a trademark of National Geographic Partners, LLC.

For more information, visit nationalgeographic.com, call 1-877-873-6846, or write to the following address:

National Geographic Partners
1145 17th Street N.W.
Washington, D.C. 20036-4688 U.S.A.

Visit us online at nationalgeographic.com/books

For librarians and teachers: nationalgeographic.com/books/librarians-and-educators

More for kids from National Geographic: natgeokids.com

National Geographic Kids magazine inspires children to explore their world with fun yet educational articles on animals, science, nature, and more. Using fresh storytelling and amazing photography, *Nat Geo Kids* shows kids ages 6 to 14 the fascinating truth about the world—and why they should care. **kids.nationalgeographic.com/subscribe**

For information about special discounts for bulk purchases, please contact National Geographic Books Special Sales: specialsales@natgeo.com

For rights or permissions inquiries, please contact National Geographic Books Subsidiary Rights: bookrights@natgeo.com

Designed by Eva Absher-Schantz
Codes and puzzles developed by Dr. Gareth Moore

Hardcover ISBN: 978-1-4263-3681-2
Reinforced library binding ISBN: 978-1-4263-3682-9

Printed in China
19/PPS/1

PRAISE FOR THE EXPLORER ACADEMY SERIES

"A fun, exciting, and action-packed ride that kids will love."
—**J.J. Abrams,** award-winning film and
television creator, writer, producer, and director

"Inspires the next generation of curious kids to go out into our world and discover something unexpected."
—**James Cameron,** National Geographic
Explorer-in-Residence and acclaimed filmmaker

"...a fully packed high-tech adventure that offers both cool, educational facts about the planet and a diverse cast of fun characters."
—*Kirkus Reviews*

"Thrill-seeking readers are going to love Cruz and his friends and want to follow them on every step of their high-tech, action-packed adventure."
—**Lauren Tarshis,** author of the I Survived series

"Absolutely brilliant! Explorer Academy is a fabulous feast for mind and heart—a thrilling, inspiring journey with compelling characters, wondrous places, and the highest possible stakes. Just as there's only one planet Earth, there's only one series like this. Don't wait another instant to enjoy this phenomenal adventure!"
—**T.A. Barron,** author of the Merlin Saga

"Nonstop action and a mix of full-color photographs and drawings throughout make this appealing to aspiring explorers and reluctant readers alike, and the cliffhanger ending ensures they'll be coming back for more."
—*School Library Journal*

"Explorer Academy is sure to awaken readers' inner adventurer and curiosity about the world around them. But you don't have to take my word for it—check out Cruz, Emmett, Sailor, and Lani's adventures for yourself!"
—**LeVar Burton,** actor, director, author, and host
of the PBS children's series *Reading Rainbow*

"Sure to appeal to kids who love code cracking and mysteries with cutting-edge technology."
—*Booklist*

"I promise: Once you enter Explorer Academy, you'll never want to leave."
—**Valerie Tripp,** co-creator and author
of the American Girl series

"...the book's real strength rests in its adventure, as its heroes...tackle puzzles and simulated missions as part of the educational process. Maps, letters, and puzzles bring the exploration to life, and back matter explores the 'Truth Behind the Fiction'... This exciting series...introduces young readers to the joys of science and nature."
—*Publishers Weekly*

"Both my 8-year-old girl and 12-year-old boy LOVED this book. It's fun and adventure and mystery all rolled into one."
—**Mom blogger,** Beckham Project

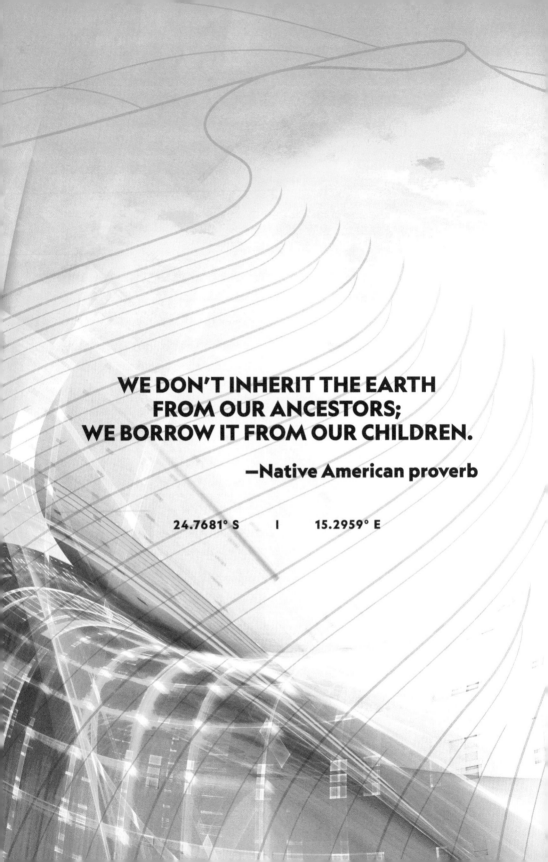

**WE DON'T INHERIT THE EARTH
FROM OUR ANCESTORS;
WE BORROW IT FROM OUR CHILDREN.**

—Native American proverb

24.7681° S | 15.2959° E

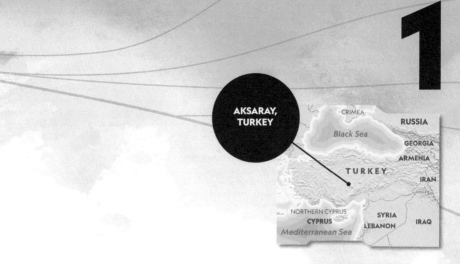

A DROP OF WATER

splashed onto Cruz's forehead.

"Emmett," he moaned, feeling the bead roll down his temple. "One more minute."

Cruz was drifting off again, when another drop tapped him on the bridge of his nose. "Okay, okay." His roommate was right. They'd be in big trouble if they were late to class. Cruz yawned, his eyelids fluttering. "You win, Emmett. I'm…" The creamy white ceiling he expected to see was, instead, a forbidding black hole. "…up," he gulped.

He remembered now. Cruz was not in his soft, warm bed in cabin 202 on board *Orion*, Explorer Academy's flagship vessel. Not even close. He was huddled at the bottom of a cold, damp cave somewhere outside of Aksaray, Turkey. Cruz's neck was tipped back. His head, rather than being cradled in his cloud of a pillow, was awkwardly butted up against unforgiving rock. The last thing he recalled before falling asleep was peering up into the stone well he'd fallen down. Cruz had scanned the void for any hint of light, any sign that help was on the way. He had seen only darkness then. And now.

"*Achoo!*" With the sneeze, Cruz's head snapped forward. A cramp shot through his neck. "Ow!" he yelped, and his cry echoed back to him. "Ow… ow… ow."

Cruz scooted out from under the dribble of water. Bones lay

5

scattered around him like driftwood on the beach after a storm. The good news was they no longer frightened him. At first, coming face-to-skull with a dozen or so skeletons *had* freaked him out. To get his heart to stop trying to leap out of his chest, Cruz had told himself it wasn't so bad. He would have been excited to uncover even a tiny piece of bone near the surface, so there was no reason to panic over finding a bunch of them so far below it, right? That sounded good. Plus, it had kept his heart where it belonged.

Once Cruz realized he had survived the tumble into the cave, his first impulse had been to reach into the upper pocket of his uniform for Mell, his honeybee drone. She could fly to the surface for help. Unfortunately, his pocket was empty. He'd left the little drone back on *Orion*. Mell was on a mission of her own. A few weeks back, Bryndis had shown him a blue door she'd discovered on the lowest deck of the ship. Cruz had left Mell perched above the mystery door to record anyone entering or leaving the room. Soon after, the drone had captured Jericho Miles on video. It was quite a surprise to Cruz. Jericho was a tech who worked in the top secret Synthesis lab in the basement of the Academy. So what was he doing on board *Orion*? Emmett had said it probably wasn't anything to worry about, reasoning that Explorer Academy was the perfect cover for the Synthesis to travel the world and conduct classified research. Still, Cruz couldn't shake the feeling that something else was going on.

Cruz glanced at the clock on his school-issued Organic Synchronization wristband (aka the Open Sesame passkey band). The thin gold screen read 3:12 a.m. Seriously?

He'd been stuck here for 11 hours! The numbers were flickering. The mini solar-powered computer must be losing juice. Cruz let out a ragged breath. So far, his attempts to contact the surface had failed.

Cruz tapped his communications pin. "Cruz Coronado to Marisol Coronado."

He got no response from his aunt.

Numb fingertips touched the pin again. "Cruz to Emmett Lu?"

Again, nothing. Cruz tried the rest of his teammates—Sailor York, Bryndis Jónsdóttir, and Dugan Marsh. No answer.

Before his mishap, Cruz had been on an archaeological mission with the rest of the explorers. It had begun as a class assignment on board *Orion*. Team Cousteau—Cruz's team—had been scouring satellite images looking for looting pits, when they'd come across the outline of an unknown archaeological feature. Thinking they may have stumbled onto an ancient tomb or temple, Aunt Marisol and Dr. Luben had led all 23 explorers to the actual location in Turkey. Cruz had been excavating alongside his teammates, when he'd broken away to check out an out-crop. The rest was blurry. One minute he was examining prehistoric art on the wall of a cave, and the next he was plunging down a hole. Still, Cruz was lucky. His OS band indicated he'd suffered only a slight concussion and minor bruises. It could have been worse. Had he landed a few feet to the left, he would have hit solid rock instead of hard-packed dirt.

Cruz suddenly sat up. There had been something else, too...before the fall. A jolt. It hadn't come from beneath him, not like an earthquake or a landslide. It was more like...

Pressure. Yes. When he'd leaned into the space to look down, Cruz had felt a pressure between his shoulder blades. The fog of uncertainty was beginning to clear. His fall was no accident. He'd been pushed! And there was no doubt in Cruz's mind who was behind it: Nebula. Several weeks ago, he'd received an anonymous note warning him that Nebula's spies were out to steal the journal and kill him before he turned 13. Yet, Cruz still had the journal safely tucked in the upper-left pocket of his jacket. And today was November 29—his 13th birthday.

"You're zero for two, Nebula," Cruz shouted into the empty cavern. "I'm still alive!" "Alive … ive … ive," proudly proclaimed his echo.

But for how long?

This was not how he'd planned to spend his birthday. His father would be calling. Maybe he'd already tried. Cruz sure wished he could talk to his dad. His mom, too. But only one of those things was truly possible. He wondered if his dad had gotten him the new hover surfboard he'd been asking for. Okay, begging for. Cruz gazed at his stone prison. Home felt like a galaxy away.

It was his own fault. Cruz had broken the two most important rules of exploring. Rule number one: Never go by yourself. Rule number two: Always tell your expedition leader where you're headed. Cruz had done neither of those things. Dr. Luben had been the one to first point out the unusual cave to Cruz. Cruz's only hope was that the visiting instructor would remember doing so and lead the team to the cave. It was a long shot, but it was all he had.

Cruz slid over a bit farther to avoid the dripping water, which was now a steady trickle. Listening to the water was making him thirsty. He wished he could put his mouth under the flow but knew better. The water might contain bacteria, parasites, or chemicals. If only he had his aluminum bottle and survival kit, he could purify it. However, the bottle, along with his phone, tablet, and the rest of his gear were all in his backpack. Cruz had no clue where that was—maybe snagged on one of the pointed rocks that had jabbed him as he'd tumbled into the cave.

A powerful rumble came from the pit of his stomach. How long could he survive without food and water? Emmett would likely know the answer to that (probably to the minute). Cruz knew the more general one. Without fresh water, he could survive three to four days. Four days of sitting here waiting to die? No thanks.

Before falling asleep, Cruz had searched the well for an escape tunnel. He'd found nothing, but he'd been sore and dazed then. He might have missed something. Getting on all fours, Cruz began to crawl around the perimeter of the cave. He went much slower this time, probing every inch. There *had* to be a way out.

"Or not." He grimaced, gently rolling a skull out of his path.

About halfway around the well, he noticed a pile of rocks stacked up against the curved wall. They might be blocking an outlet. Cruz began to move the basketball-size stones, one by one. He got into a rhythm. Bend, lift, turn, toss. Bend, lift, turn, toss.

Ten minutes later, Cruz was huffing and about to take a break, when he realized his shoes were wet. Water was seeping through the space he was making. If water was getting in, that meant...

A way out! Cruz picked up the pace. He moved several more rocks, then, hunching his shoulders, he wriggled into the opening. There were only more rocks ahead of him. It was a dead end. A very wet dead end.

Reversing course, Cruz scrambled to put the stones back into place, packing them in as tightly as he could. But he couldn't keep the flow of water from gushing in. The grotto was quickly beginning to fill. Cruz had to get to higher ground. He hopped onto the only thing he could find: a rocky shelf about three feet tall. It was barely big enough to stand on. His heels hanging off the edge and his chin inches from the wall, Cruz searched for a route up so he could climb if he had to. And pretty soon he had to.

Cruz found a couple of toeholds but had a tougher time spotting grips for his hands. It was impossible to lean back *and* remain on the little ledge. Cruz reached over his head as water sloshed into his shoes. Blindly, he slapped at the stone. He was running out of time. Cruz went up on his toes, his hands pawing for a bump or notch or cranny or something to grab on to. He found nothing. The water was rising quickly... to his ankles... his calves...

Cruz kept slapping at the cave wall, the coarse rock shredding the skin on his fingers.

There! A knot! Not a big one, but big enough. With the water level at his knees, Cruz curled both hands around the bulge. He lifted his right foot, wedged it into the toehold, and pulled himself up. Raising his left foot, he placed it where he thought the crevice should be but hit only flat

9

rock. Cruz moved his foot up, searching. He tried making small circles but couldn't find the gap. His fingers were cramping. Ugh! Where was it? His knuckles were slipping. If he didn't find a space soon, he was going to lose his...

"Arrggh!"

Cruz toppled backward, sending up a giant splash. He was back where he'd started. Cruz slapped the water in frustration. Five seconds later, he was on his feet again. Fortunately, *Orion*'s science tech lab chief, Fanchon Quills, had designed their uniforms to be waterproof, but Cruz had a feeling Fanchon hadn't expected he would have to swim in the thing. In another few minutes, however, that's exactly what he was going to have to do. He zipped his upper-left pocket, where he kept his mother's holo-journal, then made sure the lower-right pocket was tightly closed, too. It contained his octopod. Both pockets were watertight, thank goodness.

Closing the collar of his uniform, Cruz felt something scrape the back of his neck. He reached behind him, his fingers closing around a metal tab. That's right! Every explorer's jacket was equipped with two critical survival items: a parachute, which wouldn't help him here, and a flotation device, which most definitely would! Except Cruz wasn't sure how to inflate the thing. He could almost hear his adviser, Taryn Secliff, say, *You'd know what to do if you hadn't glossed over the uniform instruction manual.*

"I know, Taryn, I know..." Cruz yanked open his belt and unzipped his jacket. Wrestling free of the sleeves, he whipped the coat inside out. He found a small tab near the collar. It was engraved with a *P*—for "parachute," no doubt. Okay, so where was the one for the float? Frantically, he went down the lining, searching for an *F* tab. He didn't find one. Cruz moaned. "How in the world am I supposed to activate this dumb flotation device?"

"Personal flotation device deployment confirmed." The calm female voice startled him. It was Fanchon!

"Cruz Coronado, please prepare for PFD deployment," said Fanchon. Her instructions were coming from his OS band! Smart. Connecting his uniform to his personal computer gave him, and only him, access to and control of his gear. He should have known when all else failed, he could count on his OS band for help.

What did Fanchon mean by "prepare"? He was about to ask, when the computerized Fanchon instructed, "Please fully secure jacket, pockets, and cuffs. Beginning ten-second countdown sequence now. Ten...nine... eight..."

"Hold on!" Cruz threw his jacket over his shoulders and shoved his arms into his sleeves. The water was edging up past his knees. A current was beginning to form. He had to take a wider stance to remain upright in the swirling water.

"Six...five..."

Cruz yanked the buckles tight on the bottom of each sleeve, then jerked the zipper on the front of his jacket up so hard he was sure he'd broken it.

"Two...one," said Fanchon. "PFD activation commencing."

The hem of Cruz's jacket tightened against his hips. His cuffs and collar were sealing, too. A sudden rush of air down his back sent a chill through him. Cruz watched his sleeves slowly swell. As they did, his arms rose from his sides. His chest was puffing up, too. His jacket took less than 15 seconds to fully inflate. He felt like a giant marshmallow.

The water was still rising...up to his hips...his stomach...his ribs...

Once the water level reached his chest, Cruz lifted his feet to test if the float could hold him. It did! He was buoyant. As the floodwaters inched upward, they took Cruz with them. It was strange to be going back up the very hole that had brought him down here, but at least he was moving in a better direction. Cruz wasn't sure how far he had fallen into the shaft. He strained, looking for the gap in the rock he had fallen through.

Uh-oh. Trouble ahead. Cruz was heading for an opening on the opposite side of the cave wall. No! He needed to go up, not down. Kicking, he thrashed his arms to steer away from the hole, but the current was too strong. He was going in! The force of the tide spun him through

the opening, tipping him to one side. Water went up his nose and down his throat. Cruz came up coughing, trying to spit out water while gulping in air.

When he could see again, Cruz realized he was riding the rapids through a narrow tunnel. Of course! This must be a lava tube. Once the water had risen to the level of the tube, he'd been dumped into the passage like a helpless spider down a bathtub drain. The river was powerful and choppy. It was like rafting on the wildest white water imaginable, except *Cruz* was the raft. The swift flow tossed him from one side of the tube to the other.

Bouncing from wall to wall, Cruz quickly saw he wasn't out of the woods yet. About 30 yards ahead, there was a fork in the tube. The river was propelling him straight toward the wall of rock between the two paths. Which way should he go? Cruz kicked hard with his right foot and tried to row with his right arm, shooting for the left fork. This was going to be close! Turning his head, Cruz braced for impact. His shoulder smashed into a corner, but he made it into the left fork. Almost immediately, he felt the force of the water easing up. Was he slowing? Yes! The water level was dropping, too. A few hundred yards downstream, Cruz was able to touch bottom. Dragging his soles, he skidded to a stop on a sandbar. Exhausted, Cruz could only lie on the wet gravel, heaving. "Deactivate ... PFD."

"Confirmed. PFD deflating," came Fanchon's muffled voice from inside his puffed jacket. Cruz shivered as air escaped from vents in his collar, cuffs, and coattail. "Warning!" said Fanchon. "Organic Synchronization band detecting elevated heart rate, elevated body temperature, inadequate caloric intake, inadequate hydration, electrolyte imbalance—"

"Yeah, yeah," groaned Cruz. "OS band, switch to data readout."

"Confirmed."

Cruz usually kept his OS band stats on "readout" rather than "spoken." In all of the jostling, he must have hit the command on his touch screen. His coat returning to its original form, Cruz rolled onto his side. His legs felt like concrete blocks. His arms, too. Even his eyes were sore.

Everything was going in and out of focus.

He squinted. Was that a ...?

Snake! Cruz popped up. Thrusting his hands out behind him, he did a crab walk at world-record pace, traveling backward over the gravel and dirt as fast as his hands and feet could take him. The only thing that stopped him was the cave wall. His blood pounded in his ears. With trembling fingers, Cruz reached to unzip the pocket that held his octopod. One spritz was enough to paralyze a human for a good 15 minutes. He hoped it would have the same effect on big black poisonous snakes. Cruz fumbled for the ball. He took aim. The snake had slithered around a carved stone post ...

Wait. A *carved* post? In a cave?

"Light on, full power," he whispered into his OS band. Cruz knew the device didn't have much power left, but he *had* to see this.

As the beam from his OS band gradually illuminated his surroundings, Cruz's jaw dropped. Beyond the snake, which, as luck would have it, was stone, stood a maze of crumbling buildings. An ancient city! Was this real?

Slowly rising, Cruz's wobbly legs took him toward the sprawling

honeycomb of attached structures. A few of the rectangular mud-brick walls remained intact, but many had collapsed. Cruz was able to step over many of the walls. Most of the rooms were the same size and shape. The walls had been coated with plaster and smoothed down, their surfaces decorated with red-and-black geometric paintings of humans, flowers, and animals—birds, bears, leopards, dogs, and cattle. One wall in particular caught his eye. Mounted at shoulder level were the thick horns of a bull or an ox. Cruz wasn't sure about the species, but he knew the technique, all right. "Bucranium," he murmured.

It was a term he'd learned from Aunt Marisol. Bucranium was an art form dating back to the Stone Age. People covered the skulls and horns of large animals with plaster, then hung the pieces in their homes and temples. His aunt had told him that sometimes, bucrania surrounded a burial place, a symbolic way to protect it from harm. Cruz only knew bucrania from the postcards Aunt Marisol used to send him. He had never before seen it in person. Cruz went in for a closer look at the smooth, pale white horns.

Cruz continued on and, barely a few steps later, saw a glint in the rubble. He picked up a figurine no bigger than his palm. He dusted it off.

It looked like a deer, though it might be a horse. It was hard to tell, its features dulled and worn by time. The deer was unpainted. Its head looked curiously outward, and a tiny black eye sparkled. Obsidian, he'd bet. Thousands of years ago, the sharp volcanic glass rock would have been used for all kinds of things, from weapons to tools to art. The deer's other eye was missing its gem. Curling the deer into his palm, Cruz continued carefully picking his way through the ruins. On the outer edge of the labyrinth, the cave ceiling sloped downward, crushing a tall, circular stone structure. Whatever it was—a temple or theater—was buried under tons of dirt and rock. Cruz could see only a few feet of a curved wall. Could this be the feature Cruz had spotted on the satellite map, the one that had brought the explorers out here?

If it was, that meant...

He had done it! Cruz had found the site the explorers had been searching for! He threw his head back. "Wahoo!" His voice was still echoing through the stone chamber when his OS light went out. Cruz was in the dark. Again. Shortest celebration in history.

Okay, so he'd made the archaeological discovery of a lifetime, but what would it matter if *his* lifetime ended here? Cruz sank to the ground. He balanced the deer on his knee and waited for his eyes to adjust. His stomach was demanding food again. His lips were dry, his throat parched. The inside of his head felt like a cotton ball, all fuzzy and soft.

He would close his eyes. For a minute.

One minute became two, two became three...

Cruz heard a noise. It sounded like static and was coming from his OS band.

"Em...to...onado."

"Emmett?" Cruz's eyelids flew open. "Emmett, it's Cruz! It's me. I'm here! *I'm here!* Can you hear me?"

He could hear cheers.

"We hear you!" called Emmett. "We've been trying to contact you for hours."

"Same here."

"Cruz, are you hurt?" It was his aunt.

Cruz tapped the health icon on his OS band.

No medical conditions to report.

Weird. Hadn't his band said he'd had a concussion and a hairline fracture of the right big toe earlier? The OS band must have been malfunctioning. Or he had been dreaming the whole thing.

"No, I'm … I'm fine, Aunt Marisol," said Cruz. A noise came from his belly that sounded like an airplane taking off. "Okay, maybe a little hungry and tired but otherwise all right. How did you find me?"

"I tracked your location through your OS band," said Emmett.

Cruz clasped his hands. *Thank you, OS band!*

"It took me forever to lock on to you," said Emmett. "You must have been moving around a little."

Cruz snorted. "Yeah, a little."

"It looks like you're within a half mile of a ground-level opening," said Emmett.

"I am? I'm in the dark. Which way should I go to get out of—"

"Don't," ordered Emmett. "I don't want to lose your signal again. Stay put."

"We're going to hike in." That was Dugan.

"We've got supplies," added Sailor. "We're bringing food, water, blankets, and first aid gear. Do you need anything else?"

"No." His teammates were all he needed.

"I'll call your dad," said Aunt Marisol. "Sit tight. We'll be there as soon as we can."

"Okay. Cruz, out."

"Wait, Cruz! I … we almost forgot," said Emmett. "There's one more thing …"

What was wrong *now*? "Yeah?"

"Happy birthday!" came the chorus from his fellow explorers.

Cruz managed a grin. It may not have been the birthday he'd planned on, but it was certainly one he'd never forget.

2

►HEARING A CHIME, *Thorne*

Prescott reached for his phone.

He drew in a sharp breath. This was it—the note he had been waiting for from Zebra. By now, it was all over. The cipher was in Nebula's hands and Cruz Coronado had finally been taken care of. His index finger poised above the message icon, Prescott didn't know why he hesitated. Wasn't this what he'd wanted—an end to this whole ugly chapter?

Absolutely.

Prescott touched the screen.

Assignment FAILED.

CC is still alive. He's like a cat with nine lives.

Lion wasn't happy. He thinks we may be too

late. There's only one way to know for sure.

How many lives can the cat have left?

Will handle things from here.

Zebra

Unbelievable. Still, you did have to admire someone who didn't give up, even when he had no chance of winning. Cruz was a fighter. Prescott liked that. He was a fighter, too. Of course, only one of them could come out on top, and Prescott had no intention of losing.

Prescott read the note again. What did Zebra mean, they were too late? Also, it was rather bold of Zebra to make a new plan without clearing it with him first. Too bold. Prescott was in charge of this operation. Wasn't he?

It was quite possible that Brume had lost confidence in him. And no wonder. Prescott had certainly made a mess of things. He had missed too many chances—first to handle Cruz in Hawaii, then again in D.C., and, finally, to kidnap Cruz's father. Prescott didn't know how that had gone off the rails, but he was the guy in charge. If things went wrong, it was his fault.

It wasn't like him to make mistakes. He knew better. He'd learned a long time ago not to let emotions or attachments interfere with work. It's why Brume trusted him. It's also why Aubrie left him. She deserved better anyway. Prescott shook her image from his head. There was business to attend to.

He typed a single word into his phone and sent the question to Zebra:

How?

Seconds later, the reply came. It, too, was one word:

Poison.

3

ANTALYA,
TURKEY

ROMANIA   CRIMEA
                        RUSSIA
BULGARIA   *Black Sea*
                        GEORGIA
                        ARMENIA
            T U R K E Y   IRAN

NORTHERN CYPRUS
        CYPRUS   SYRIA
Mediterranean Sea LEBANON   IRAQ

EW. Was that what he thought it was? Cruz dipped his chin. It
was. A sleeping Sailor had left a puddle of drool on his shoulder. She was
snoring, too, letting out a tiny pig grunt each time she exhaled.

"Sailor." He gently shrugged to wake her.

"One more minute, Mum," she mumbled, flipping toward the window.

On his other side, Dugan was twitching in his sleep. He'd elbowed Cruz
in the side at least half a dozen times. Sandwiched between his two
teammates in the self-driving SUV for the better part of four hours,
Cruz had gotten little rest himself. For the last hour, he'd been listening
to the *ka-tunk, ka-tunk* drone of the windshield wipers as they whisked
away a light drizzle. All of the explorers, along with Aunt Marisol, were
caravanning to the port city of Antalya, Turkey, to meet *Orion*. Cruz and
his teammates were in the lead car of three. Lined with palm trees, the
long, straight road hugged the shoreline of the Mediterranean Sea.
Peering through the front seats, Cruz watched the computerized map
on the dash track their position. The blue car was closing in on the
blinking green star that marked their destination: the harbor. It
wouldn't be long now. Cruz could hardly wait to get back to the ship.

It had been eight days since Cruz's cave mishap. Seven of those days
had been spent excavating the Stone Age settlement. Once the explorers had found Cruz and knew he was all right, they had gotten busy
unearthing, documenting, and photographing the ancient city's many

treasures. They discovered grave sites, pottery, tools, weapons, jewelry, paintings, and art (including more bucrania). Soon, Aunt Marisol and Professor Luben had announced the dig was over, even though it seemed as if they had barely scratched the surface. As everyone gathered near the amphitheater at the end of the day, Cruz had pleaded the explorers' case to their instructors. "We can't go now. We're still finding incredible artifacts. Look!" He turned to Dugan, who was carefully dusting off an oblong cuff bracelet carved from animal bone.

"You've all done a superb job," said Professor Luben, his eyes roving over the tired faces circling him. "But it's time to go. That's the nature of archaeology. Scientists often run out of money, manpower, time, or any and all of the above. It's not uncommon to have to come back at a later date or turn things over to others."

"Maybe we can make arrangements to return next year," added Aunt Marisol. "For now, explorers, we need to get back to the ship. Trust me, your site *is* in good hands. Professor Luben is going to stay behind to coordinate a multi-university excavation team."

Twenty-three heads swung to Professor Luben.

"You're really not coming back to *Orion* with us?" asked Felipe.

Their substitute teacher shook his head. "You already have an anthropology instructor, remember?" He nodded to Cruz's aunt. "Now that she's back, it's time for me to move on to my next adventure. Not to worry. Something tells me I'll be seeing you again on your travels."

The explorers tried to look cheerful, though everyone was disappointed. Cruz was glad to have his aunt home but, like his classmates, he was going to miss Professor Luben.

"Still doesn't seem right," grumbled Sailor, "letting other people dig at *our* site."

Everyone murmured in agreement.

"I know," said Aunt Marisol sympathetically. Yet, Cruz noticed that the corners of her mouth had turned up. She was clearly pleased to see that her students had caught the archaeology bug, as she called it.

As the self-driving SUV rolled down the highway, Cruz slipped a hand

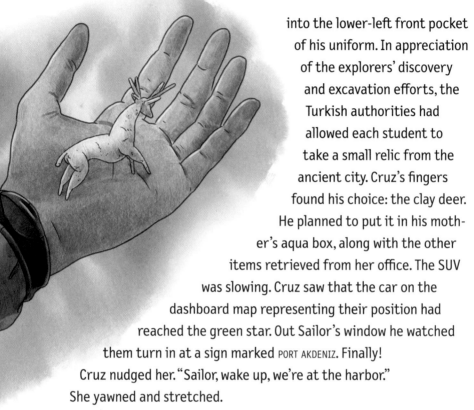

into the lower-left front pocket of his uniform. In appreciation of the explorers' discovery and excavation efforts, the Turkish authorities had allowed each student to take a small relic from the ancient city. Cruz's fingers found his choice: the clay deer. He planned to put it in his mother's aqua box, along with the other items retrieved from her office. The SUV was slowing. Cruz saw that the car on the dashboard map representing their position had reached the green star. Out Sailor's window he watched them turn in at a sign marked PORT AKDENIZ. Finally!

Cruz nudged her. "Sailor, wake up, we're at the harbor."

She yawned and stretched.

The tires of the SUV had barely rolled to a stop, when Cruz reached over Sailor and threw open the door. Yawning again, she almost rolled out of the car. Cruz caught her before she did. Sailor planted both feet on the concrete and eased herself up. The rain was letting up, though the afternoon sky was still the color of wet cement. Stretching her arms up, Sailor arched her back. Cruz scrambled out of the vehicle, his eyes rapidly sweeping over the row of fishing, tour, and pleasure boats moored at the pier. There! The deep-blue hull, the sparkling white decks, the black-and-yellow flag billowing in the stiff Mediterranean breeze. *Orion!*

Home!

Cruz was the first explorer to grab his backpack and duffel from the trunk. He made a beeline for the pier, rushing across the wooden planks like a little kid. He could hardly wait to see Taryn and Hubbard. He'd sure missed that pup—

"Oops, sorry!" Taking the sharp turn on the L-shaped dock, Cruz had nearly mowed down a thin older man. He was wearing a light blue beret and a tattered jean jacket and had several cameras slung around his neck.

"*Sorun değil,*" said the man. "No problem. Are you one of the student explorers?"

"Yes, I'm headed to that ship." Cruz tried to step around, but the man moved with him, blocking his path.

"Which one of you discovered the Stone Age civilization?"

"Uh...I guess that would be me, but we all excavated the site."

Lifting his camera, the guy snapped his photo.

Cruz stepped back, uncomfortable that someone he didn't know had taken his picture. A group of adults who'd been hovering near *Orion*'s gangway were now suddenly hurrying down the pier toward him. As they closed in, Cruz saw cameras and video gear. Reporters! The dock swayed under all that weight in motion. Backing up, Cruz glanced over his shoulder. Everyone was sure taking their time getting their gear out of the car.

The pack of reporters flocked to Cruz like hungry seagulls to a bag of french fries. Cruz was trapped. He couldn't move to either side. He couldn't move forward. And if he took one more step back, he'd be in the water! Microphones were thrust in his face. Lights blinded him.

"Is it true you uncovered the oldest Stone Age settlement in the region—even older than Çatalhöyük?" asked a woman.

"How old is it?" shot out a man before Cruz could answer.

"How old are *you*?" asked another reporter.

Cruz could feel his heels slip off the edge of the pier. "Me?...I'm twelve, I mean thirteen—"

"How did you find it?"

"Did you bring any relics back with you?"

"Do you want to be an archaeologist when you grow up?"

Cruz broke out in a cold sweat. "Uh...sorry...what was the first question again?"

"Whoa! Coming through! Make a hole, people!"

At the sight of his resident adviser swimming through the crowd, Cruz let out the biggest, most grateful sigh ever. "Taryn!"

"Some welcome, huh? Looks like news travels faster than explorers. Relax, I'll handle this." Putting up a hand, Taryn faced the mob. "Archaeology professor Dr. Marisol Coronado will be here in a few moments to answer all of your questions and maybe—*maybe*—allow a student to be interviewed as well. You, there! What is with that light?" She shaded her eyes. "Are you trying to signal Mars or something?"

The light went out.

"Thank you," said Taryn.

Behind him, Cruz could hear footsteps clomping on wood. The dock wobbled. With Taryn in charge, Cruz felt brave enough to move sideways through the reporters to join Aunt Marisol and the rest of his class.

"Is all this for us?" asked Bryndis, ice blue eyes widening.

"They heard about our discovery," said Cruz.

"Sweet as! We're going to be on the news!" proclaimed Sailor, running her hands through her bangs. Each fingernail was painted a different color.

After briefly chatting with Taryn, Cruz's aunt turned to her students. "Is there an explorer who would like to answer a few questions from the media?"

Team Cousteau put their heads together. Cruz knew he was the obvious choice, but he didn't want to make it seem like his aunt was playing favorites. "You should do it," Cruz whispered to Dugan. "You found those cool animal relief carvings on the temple."

"Yeah, but you found the whole *city*," replied Dugan.

"But you were the one who convinced Team Magellan to go to Turkey after they won the maze challenge. If it weren't for you, they would have chosen Egypt."

"But if it weren't for you pointing out the anomaly on the satellite image, I never would have had to talk Team Magellan into—"

"I'll do it, Professor Coronado!" belted out Matteo.

"Thank you, Matteo." Aunt Marisol motioned for him to join her. "The rest of you may board the ship."

As the other explorers wove through the pack of journalists, Team Cousteau stood there, gaping.

"What just happened?" choked Sailor.

"Gotta be quick on your feet to beat Team Magellan," teased Ali, passing them.

"He's right," muttered Emmett, his emoto-glasses becoming long rectangles the color of dirt. "We took too long to decide."

There was nothing Team Cousteau could do but grab their bags and follow their classmates. Trudging down the pier next to the ship, Cruz glanced up. He could see the veranda of the corner cabin he shared with Emmett. Good old *Orion*. The flagship of the Academy's fleet was always reliable, always the same. Well, almost always. Cruz noticed the helicopter that usually sat on the top deck was gone.

Dugan led them up the gangway. They could hear Aunt Marisol. She was using her teacher voice with the reporters. "This adventure began because some of our explorers were searching satellite images looking for looting pits. Their keen eyes noticed outlines of perfect circles on the ground—shapes they'd learned are not typically found in nature. Like all good explorers, they were curious about these features that appeared to be human-made ..."

"Those curious explorers with the keen eyes would be *us*," growled Sailor. "Team Cousteau."

"We should be the ones being interviewed," said Emmett.

Ahead, Dugan had dropped his head so far Cruz could barely see it attached to his neck.

"Oh well," sighed Cruz. "It's probably for the local news anyway."

Two hours later, 23 explorers were in the third-floor lounge to watch a beaming Matteo Montefiore on the *national* newscast.

"Excavating the cave was tough," said the Matteo on the screen. "It was a long hike in over some rough terrain, but we couldn't give up. I mean, how many times in your life do you get to discover a city that's more than ten thousand years old? I still can't believe it."

"Neither can I," mumbled Sailor. "Geez, you'd think he discovered and excavated the site all by himself."

Felipe turned the channel. A still photo of Matteo smirking was hovering above the news anchor's shoulder. Another click and there was Matteo again...

"It's a top story all around the world," said Bryndis. She was scrolling through her tablet. "New York, London, Tokyo, Sydney..."

"Can we get dinner before I lose my appetite?" asked Dugan.

"You're going to eat *with us*?" blurted Sailor.

"Why not?"

"You always eat with Team Mag—"

"Not tonight," clipped Dugan.

The news over, the explorers began drifting away. As Matteo passed him, Cruz said, as sincerely as he could, "Good interview." He didn't want to be a bad sport.

"Thanks," said Matteo. "I...um...you know, said a bunch more stuff... and talked about you guys finding the site, but they cut that part out."

Cruz nodded. His teammates nodded. Matteo nodded. He had a weird look on his face, though, like when your milk tastes funny. Or your shirt is itchy. Or you've just told one monster of a lie.

"I...uh...gotta go," said Matteo, trotting away.

"Awk-ward," sang Sailor, chewing on a purple pinkie nail.

"I wonder if this is how the Pinzón brothers felt," said Emmett as they made their way to the dining room.

Bryndis wrinkled her nose. "Who?"

"Exactly."

"The Pinzón brothers captained the *Niña* and the *Pinta* on Columbus's first voyage to America," explained Dugan. "Now they're all but forgotten by history."

Cruz understood why everyone was irritated—he was, too—but he didn't want to stew in it. This was the kind of thing that could get under your skin, if you let it. It might even affect their performance as a team.

They had to let it go. Cruz spun to walk backward in front of his friends. "Okay, maybe Matteo threw us under the Christopher Colum-*bus*…"

Everyone groaned, but they were half grinning, too.

"*But,*" Cruz continued, "in all fairness, Team Magellan *is* the reason we were able to go to Turkey in the first place. We found the Stone Age city, and that's what matters—not who gets the credit, right?"

"Right," muttered his teammates with about as much enthusiasm as dead earthworms.

Joining the buffet line in the dining room, Cruz furrowed his brow. Something about Dugan was different. The old Dugan would have piped up to Aunt Marisol that he'd do the interview the second she'd asked for volunteers or, at the very least, would have grumbled about how unfairly Team Cousteau had been treated. The new Dugan seemed unsure. Worried. Distracted. Maybe it had something to do with what Dugan had told Cruz in Barcelona, that he might have to leave the Academy. At the time, that was all Dugan had been able to say. Or had wanted to say. Cruz had tried to bring up the subject with him a few times since but didn't know how to start the conversation. Was it grades? Was he homesick? Was it the team? Whatever was going on, Cruz figured Dugan would tell him when he was ready.

"Lasagna night!" cheered Emmett, peering around the explorers in front of them.

Lasagna was Emmett's favorite, which meant he'd have seconds and thirds and maybe fourths. Cruz picked up a tray.

"Taryn Secliff to Cruz Coronado."

Cruz tapped his badge. "Cruz here."

"Can you please report to my cabin?"

"Now? I'm about to—"

"Yes, please." She didn't sound mad, but she didn't sound happy, either.

"Be right there." Cruz put his tray back on the stack. He turned to his friends. "Catch you later."

A visit with Taryn meant he'd get to see Hubbard. Cruz played fetch with the friendly Westie pup as often as possible. The two also shared a secret. Hubbard was carrying Cruz's mom's formula. All three of the interlocking stones that Cruz had found so far were tucked into a zippered pocket of the dog's life vest. With Nebula after him, it was too dangerous for Cruz to wear the cipher around his neck as he had done initially. His cabin wasn't safe, either. It had already been ransacked once. Although his aunt had encouraged him to put the cipher in the ship's vault, Cruz couldn't bring himself to do it.

He scurried down the winding staircase, turning left in the lower level of the atrium to head to the back of the ship. Taryn's cabin was the first one on the port side of the explorers' passage. Her door was slightly open. He knocked. No one answered.

"Taryn?"

No reply. An uneasy feeling swept through him. Taryn was not a practical joker. She wouldn't call him down here only to suddenly vanish. Cruz stretched out a hand. He lightly tapped the door. It opened a few inches farther. The hinges creaked, sending a wicked chill up his spine. He didn't like this. Not one bit.

"Hubbard?" Cruz's voice was a mouse squeak.

When the little white dog didn't come bounding toward him, Cruz took a hesitant step inside the cabin. Then another. Ears alert, Cruz heard only the low pulse of the engines. Maybe he should get a security guard?

He leaned, cautiously peering around the corner. What he saw made him jump back. It couldn't be. It. Could. Not. Be!

"Lani?"

4

"BET YOU WEREN'T

expecting me!" Lani Kealoha bounced on her toes.

Cruz shook his head. He was in shock.

Lani wasn't his only surprise. Next to her stood the president of Explorer Academy, Dr. Regina Hightower! Cruz rushed to give Lani a hug. He released her, his mind racing. What were the two of them doing here?

It had been three months since Cruz had left Lani back home in Hanalei to attend the Academy. Despite their distance, they spoke every few days, and Cruz never opened his mother's holo-journal for a new clue without Lani present on a video call. Thank goodness, too, because she'd been a huge help in finding the three pieces of the cipher he'd discovered so far. Also, it was Lani who'd unraveled the clues his dad had left behind after being kidnapped by Nebula. Then there was Dr. Hightower. Cruz hadn't seen her since *Orion* had set sail from the East Coast of the United States two months ago. However, he did

recall Taryn telling him that Dr. Hightower often visited the Academy ships while they were at sea to check in on the explorers. Is that what this was? A friendly visit? Or something more?

A horrible thought suddenly occurred to Cruz. "Is it my dad?" He pulled back. "Is something wrong—"

"No, no!" cried Lani. "Your dad is okay. Everything is fine. In fact, it's better than fine. It's fantastic!" She revealed a set of gleaming white teeth. "I'm joining Explorer Academy!"

Cruz's jaw fell. "No!"

"Yes!"

"How … why … when …?" he sputtered.

"It's quite simple," broke in Dr. Hightower. "Lani was at the top of our list of alternates."

"She was?" gasped Cruz. "I didn't even know there *were* alternates."

"Me either." Lani twisted the thin silver lock she had dyed into her chin-length chestnut brown hair.

"We know how disappointing it can be to come so close and not make the cut," said Dr. Hightower. "That's why it's school policy not to divulge our list of alternates to anyone. We think it's a kinder approach. Plus, it prevents us from having to deal with well-meaning but insistent parents, who don't see why we can't—"

"Make room for *one more student*," said a voice behind Cruz.

Taryn was in the doorway, a red leash tethering Hubbard to her. One look at Cruz and the Westie's tail wagged at triple speed. Taryn tipped her head down. "I think someone's been waiting for you." She bent to unclip the leash, and Hubbard bounded straight for Cruz, who fell to his knees so the pup could jump into his arms. Cruz buried his head in Hubbard's soft, curly fur. He smelled like strawberry shampoo. And bacon.

"So, do you approve of our new explorer, Cruz?" teased Taryn.

"You bet," said Cruz over Hubbard's head. "She belongs here. She always has."

"I hope I can catch up." Lani bit her lip.

"I wouldn't have asked you if I didn't have complete confidence that you could handle it," said Dr. Hightower. "My only regret is not issuing the invitation earlier. It has been a while since I let the student go whom you are replacing…"

Cruz pretended to straighten Hubbard's yellow life vest. Dr. Hightower was referring to Renshaw McKittrick, who had been expelled for cheating.

"I hesitated to issue your invite, Lani," Dr. Hightower was explaining. "I worried it might be too much to ask of you to meet the challenge of starting so late." She lifted her chin. "Then you changed my mind."

Lani put a hand to her heart. "I did?"

"Your bravery and ingenuity in rescuing Cruz's father was nothing short of remarkable. You are the kind of person we want—need—here at Explorer Academy, and I knew I could not let another day go by without giving you the opportunity to join us."

Lani gave a timid grin.

"As far as schoolwork," said Dr. Hightower, "you won't have to make up any assignments, but you will need to do some reading to catch up in your classes and go through some modified survival training with Monsieur Legrand. It's for your own safety. Even so, I've been assured that the faculty will do whatever it takes to make your transition smooth."

"I'll help, too," said Cruz. A chill went through him. "She *is* going to fill Ren's spot on Team Cousteau, isn't she, Taryn? You wouldn't switch around teams now, would you?"

His adviser tapped a red fingernail against her chin, pretending to mull it over for a few seconds. She ended his torture with a smirk. "Lani has been assigned to Team Cousteau. No sense shaking things up in the middle of the semester."

"Whew!" Cruz made a motion as if to wipe sweat from his brow.

"Now, if you'll please excuse Lani and me," said Taryn, "we have some orientation business to attend to."

"Certainly," said Dr. Hightower. She extended a hand to Lani. "Congratulations! *Fortes fortuna adiuvat.*"

"Fortune favors the brave," translated Lani, her voice cracking with emotion. "Thank you."

Cruz released the dog and stood. "Can we play with Hubbard when you're done?"

"Sure. This won't take long."

Cruz *did* want to play with Hubbard, but he also needed to retrieve the third piece of the cipher from the dog's vest. In order to unlock the next clue in his mom's journal, Cruz had to show the marble piece to the holographic image of his mother and have her confirm that it was genuine. With a grin to Lani, Cruz followed Dr. Hightower into the passageway. Taryn closed the door behind them. The head of the Academy glanced around to be sure they were alone, before whispering, "How's everything going?"

"We found the third piece of the cipher in Petra." He kept his voice low, too.

"Wonderful." She studied him. "So why do you look so worried?"

"Me? I ... I'm not worried." Cruz did not want to tell Dr. Hightower about his two recent brushes with death. First, he'd nearly been crushed by falling rocks in the city of Petra, Jordan. Thankfully, a girl—a tourist—had flung him out of the way in the nick of time. An accident? Maybe. Then there was the incident in the cave, which was definitely no accident.

The Academy president ruffled her crop of whipped-cream hair. "Cruz, perhaps it's time to consider other options."

He didn't understand. "Options?"

"Take a break."

"You want me to stop looking for the cipher!"

"Only for a little while. I fear it's getting too dangerous—"

"No." It came out harsher than he'd intended, but Cruz was not about to slow down now. Not even for a second. This was a race—he was in a race with Nebula to find and complete his mom's formula. "I'll be all right, Dr. Hightower. I've got tons of people around me: the security officers, my aunt, Sailor, Emmett, and now Lani. Geez, I've got practically a whole army."

"That's what concerns me. You're not the only one in danger. There are others involved here who have no idea the lengths Nebula will go—"

They heard a door unlock at the far end of the explorers' passage, then voices.

The Academy president lowered her head. "If you're out to win at any cost, you may find the price is higher than you ever expected to pay."

Cruz nodded.

She backed away. "Farewell, explorer."

"Bye, Dr. Hightower." Cruz watched the squared shoulders of her cream tunic jacket as she took her usual crisp, precise strides away from him. Entering the atrium, she turned to go up the grand staircase. She was probably heading up to the helicopter pad. Cruz wished she would stay a little longer. He always felt safer with Dr. Hightower around.

Taryn's cabin door opened. Lani stood there, clutching her new Academy-issued tablet and turning her left arm this way and that to examine the gold OS band now circling her wrist. Dark brown eyes looked scared. Excited, but scared. Cruz had felt the same way on his first day.

"Thanks, Ms. Secliff," said Lani.

A brown head appeared behind her. "It's Taryn. I'll bring your uniform and gear by before bedtime. Now, you're positive you don't mind not having a roommate? The other twelve girls are already paired up, but I could move someone in with you temporarily, until you get settled."

"It's fine, really," said Lani. "I have four brothers and sisters. A little

time alone will be heaven. Besides"—she threw Cruz a smirk—"it's not like I don't know anyone here."

"All right," said Taryn, "but if you get lonely or homesick—"

"I'll come by." Lani held up a hand as if to swear.

"She'll be okay, Taryn," said Cruz. "Team Cousteau will make sure of it."

"Team Cousteau," echoed Lani. "I can't believe it. I've thought about it and dreamed about it for so long. And then when you left for training I didn't think I'd ever ..."

Cruz knew, of course, that Lani had been upset when she hadn't gotten into the Academy. But he hadn't realized just how heartbroken she'd been. It had meant as much to her as it had to him. Still, she'd never wavered in her support of his achievement, even going so far as to make things for him like Mell's remote and the protective sleeve for his mom's journal. Not wanting to spoil his happiness, Lani had done a good job at hiding her own disappointment. Cruz said what he should have said to his best friend months ago. "I'm so sorry."

"I know." Her eyes misted over. "All that matters is I'm here now."

Taryn peered over Lani's head to nod to Cruz. "You want to say it?"

"No," croaked Cruz, choking back his emotions. "She should hear it from you."

Lani spun to face Taryn. "Hear what?"

Pressing her palms together, Taryn grinned. "Welcome to the Academy."

WORD THAT AN EXPLORER HAD JOINED their ranks took less than an hour to travel from bow to stern, and the explorers began crowding into cabin 214 to meet their new classmate. One by one, they introduced themselves: Zane, Ali, Matteo, Tao, Kat, Yulia, Felipe, Kwento, Misha, Weatherly, Shristine, Kendall, Femi, Emmett, Dugan, Bryndis ...

Cruz was standing in the back corner of Lani's cabin, casually leaning against the veranda door. He and Lani had decided to not let on that they'd been friends before coming to Explorer Academy. It was for Lani's own good, reasoned Cruz. Dr. Hightower's words had haunted him. He also had another reason for keeping their relationship under wraps— one he didn't reveal even to his best friend. Cruz didn't want anyone, especially Dugan, thinking that Aunt Marisol or he had any hand in Lani's acceptance into the school. She had earned her spot here. On their way to Lani's cabin, Cruz had told Emmett how he felt. His roommate had promised to keep the secret.

"I'm Bryndis ... from Iceland." The fair-haired girl eased into one of the overstuffed chairs opposite Lani, who was sitting on her bed. "I'm on Team Cousteau, too."

"Nice to meet you," said Lani. She crossed her ankles. She was wearing her favorite red-and-pink-hibiscus-print socks.

"Kealoha. Is that Hawaiian?" asked Bryndis. "Are you from Hawaii?"

"Yes and yes," said Lani.

"Dugan Marsh," drawled their other teammate, scratching the top of his crew cut. "I've never heard of anyone getting into the Academy *after* the school year started."

Lani didn't take the bait. She lifted a shoulder, as if she were as confused as everyone else.

Dugan was still eyeing her suspiciously. "You don't have any relatives that teach at the Academy, do you?"

"No," said Lani. "Do you?"

Cruz had to bite his lip to keep from grinning.

"Cruz, over there, is from Hawaii, too," said Bryndis.

"Oh, yeah?" Lani tilted her head so that she could give a wink that only Cruz could see.

Sailor bounded into the room. "Lani!"

"Uh ... hi ..." squeaked Lani, blushing. She looked up at Cruz, helpless, as Sailor jumped on the bed, flung a pair of arms around her, and squeezed.

Cruz winced. Oops. He had clued in Emmett about the situation with

Lani, but he had forgotten Sailor.

"Um...so nice to meet you," said Lani, carefully extricating herself from Sailor's death hug. "And you are...?"

"It's me—Sailor!"

"Hi...Sailor," said Lani, making eye contact. She began to slowly nod. "I just met your—our—teammates, Bryndis, Emmett, Dugan, and *Cruz*. I *just* met them."

Sailor frowned, trying to figure out what was going on. "O-kay." She bobbed her head in time with Lani's.

"Hey, explorers." Taryn poked her head in the room. "Why don't we give the new recruit a little breathing room, huh? Besides, last I checked you all have a full day of classes tomorrow. Come on, let's go..."

Everyone began filing out of Lani's cabin. As Emmett, Sailor, and Cruz strolled down the passage to cabin 202, Cruz quietly brought Sailor up to speed on the plan not to reveal to anyone that Lani and Cruz were friends before coming to the Academy.

"That's smart," said Sailor, munching on the glittery cobalt blue nail of her index finger. "But next time, tell me *before* I make an idiot out of myself, okay?"

"Gotcha."

"Sooooo," she whispered, "when are we opening the journal for the next clue?"

Cruz held his OS band up to the sensor mounted next to his cabin door. They heard the latch pop. "Now."

"But Lani—"

"Is right behind us," said Cruz, motioning with his head to the girl in the hibiscus socks hurrying down the passage toward them.

Minutes later, the four explorers were seated around the little table in Emmett and Cruz's room, as the origami journal turned into a three-dimensional, multi-pointed sphere. No matter how many times Cruz witnessed the computational transformation, it amazed him. Even though he knew there was a perfectly logical scientific explanation for it, because he had yet to fully understand the mechanics, the

whole thing felt a bit like...

Magic. Maybe it was silly, but a small part of him hoped it always did.

Cruz watched Lani. She was seeing the morphing action live for the first time.

"Wow," she gushed. "This is incredible."

"Wait a sec," whispered Emmett, "the best part is coming."

As the holographic image of his mother appeared, Lani's wide eyes grew even wider. Cruz took the third piece of the cipher from his pocket. He'd removed it from Hubbard's life vest only an hour earlier. He held the black marble triangle out to his mother. As she bent to inspect it, several locks of long, wavy blond hair fell forward. If his mom had been real or even a character in the CAVE, Cruz would have felt the sweep of her hair against his skin, but as it was, the lock passed right through his fingertips.

Petra Coronado straightened. "Well done. This is a genuine piece."

Sailor and Emmett clapped.

"Yes!" Lani pumped her fists.

Cruz let his head fall backward. The confirmation was the hardest part of the whole process. If his mom didn't authenticate a piece, they were dead in the water.

"You have unlocked a new clue," said his mother. "You'll know where to go once you solve this cryptogram."

Rows of clear three-dimensional boxes began to appear between Cruz and his mother at eye level. Like waves on a peaceful shore, they formed a slow-rolling tide. Each box was about a foot high and a foot wide. Floating inside every box was a number. Most of the boxes were clear, but a handful were brightly colored. The colorful boxes took turns sliding forward and back from their wavy rows, and as they did, Cruz heard a songbird chirping in the background. Knowing he could not memorize the cryptogram, Cruz grabbed his tablet and began recording. Thankfully, the boxes went through the routine a second time.

"There are two eights and two elevens," called Lani.

"And the numbers only go up to twenty-six," said Emmett, his glasses lime triangles.

An alphabet cipher!

"By now you've seen it thousands of times," assured his mother. "It's as familiar as a rainbow. A word of advice: Use all your senses. Good luck, Cruzer."

Cruz watched the wavy grid disappear, along with his mother's image, and a deep ache spread through his chest. He'd been wrong. Authenticating a piece of the stone cipher *was* stressful. But seeing his mom's smile fade into thin air?

That was the hardest thing of all.

5

AT THREE MINUTES after midnight, *Orion* glided away from the pier. Cruz knew the exact time the ship left Port Akdeniz because he was sitting up in bed, the only light coming from the tablet propped up against his knees. Even when his aunt used to send him postcards for fun, Cruz could never sleep when there was a cipher to crack.

At first glance, his mom's cryptogram had seemed easy—simply match every number with its corresponding letter: A = 1, B = 2, C = 3, and so on. Cruz, Emmett, Lani, and Sailor had agreed they should focus on the colorful boxed numerals that had moved toward them.

"Cruz, let's watch your video," Emmett had suggested.

"Call out the numbers, and I'll match them with the letters of the alphabet," said Sailor.

Cruz hit the playback button on his tablet, and the bird began to chirp. "The first box is red twenty-five . . . second box is green eight . . . then a purple eleven." Next came a yellow 26, an orange 11, a light blue 24, and, finally, a dark blue 8—seven boxes in all. Everyone waited as Sailor decoded the message. She took forever.

"Well?" pressed Cruz. "What does it spell?"

"Nothing," Sailor said flatly. She handed him her tablet. It was gibberish: YHKZKXH.

"It has to be *something*," said Emmett. "A person or a place . . ."

Lani was twisting her hair. "You have to be kidding."

"I'm not," insisted Emmett.

"Noooo." She laughed. "Y-H-K. I meant it could stand for *you have to be kidding.*"

"Ohhh."

They continued brainstorming for the next hour but didn't come up with anything that contained all of the letters in the code in order—or even half of them, for that matter. Everyone agreed to keep working on the cryptogram and contact Cruz if they came up with any ideas.

Readjusting his pillow, Cruz glanced at Emmett in the next bed. His roommate was conked out on his face, one arm dangling off the edge of the mattress. At least someone was getting some sleep.

Was YHKZKXH a jumble? Should he rearrange the letters? This was the order they had glided toward them, but maybe his mom had scrambled the code on purpose. Even so, with all those consonants, no matter how you moved the letters they were never going to spell a word. His mother had said that he had seen this thousands of times. If he had, he sure didn't remember where or when. Cruz stared at the screen until the letters melted together like an ice-cream sundae. He couldn't figure it out. At least, not tonight. Shutting off his tablet, Cruz slipped down beneath the covers. He tried to sleep, but even in his dreams the code haunted him. The letters and numbers sprouted legs and danced around Cruz, slipping through his fingers whenever he tried to catch them.

"Maybe we were on the wrong track," said Emmett the next morning as they headed up to class with Lani. "What if the numbers don't stand for letters? What if they're supposed to be exactly what they are?"

Cruz yawned. "You mean, like an address?"

"Or geographic coordinates."

"Or the combination to a safe," volunteered Lani.

"So *anything*," groaned Cruz.

"Keep thinking," said Lani. "We're getting closer."

Cruz hoped so. He didn't know where the ship was going, but every minute it took to unravel the clue was one more minute they might be traveling in the wrong direction.

In class, Cruz usually sat between Emmett and Sailor. However, walking into Manatee classroom, he noticed Sailor had scooted over so Lani could sit next to him. He leaned behind Lani and tapped Sailor on the shoulder. "Thanks," he mouthed.

An orange thumbnail pointed to the sky.

Bryndis and Dugan had taken their usual spots in front of them. Turning, Bryndis waved to Lani and Cruz. They waved back.

Cruz tried not to stare at Lani but couldn't help it. She looked good in her new uniform. Her hair seemed extra shiny, as if she'd brushed and brushed it. Cruz still could not believe it. His best friend was on board *Orion*. She was really *here*!

Lani caught him staring. "What? Is my GPS pin on the wrong side? Oh geez, did I get something on my jacket already? I knew I shouldn't have had pancakes and syrup—"

"No." He put a hand on her arm. "You look fine."

"Good morning, explorers!" Professor Gabriel charged into the room, his spidery legs taking long strides. His bald head glistened under the bright lights. Right behind him was Dr. Sidril Vanderwick, the assistant to *Orion*'s science tech lab chief, Fanchon Quills. Dr. Vanderwick was carrying a black box about the size of a couple of stacked bricks. As the pair went by, Emmett nudged Cruz's elbow. The explorers were going to get a cool new gadget!

Placing the black box on the front table, Dr. Vanderwick stepped back and clasped her hands neatly in front of her. Dr. Vanderwick's blondish brown hair was twisted into its usual pretzel bun. She wore her white lab coat over a white cotton shirt and a navy knee-length skirt. This time, however, instead of her white nurse's shoes, she had on a pair of canvas flats with a print of red roses—rather fancy, thought Cruz, for the scientist who rarely wore more than three solid colors and *never* anything with a pattern. Maybe Fanchon was starting to rub off on her assistant.

"Before we begin," said Professor Gabriel, "I'd like to take a moment to welcome a new explorer, Lani Kealoha from Hawaii. Aloha, Miss Kealoha!"

Everyone clapped.

"*Mahalo nui loa iā ʻoe,*" answered Lani.

"Thank you very much," said a chorus of language translators.

The explorers laughed. Lani's cheeks turned cherry red, as she realized her Hawaiian phrase had activated their automatic translators.

"A word or two is okay," Cruz whispered to her. "But any more than that and your translator will likely kick in—unless you turn it off."

"Got it."

"By now, students," continued their instructor, "you've looked out your portholes and noticed *Orion* is under way. No doubt you're wondering *where* are we heading?"

"South," shot Emmett. "We're traveling south."

"Very good, Mr. Lu," answered their instructor.

The lights dimmed. A holographic globe appeared, floating next to their teacher. With a wave of his hand, Professor Gabriel zoomed into the area around northeastern Africa and the Middle East. A red line began to extend from southern Turkey. It moved through the Mediterranean Sea, separating Egypt and Sudan from the Saudi Arabian peninsula. "Here is our route," said the professor. "We'll cruise through the Suez Canal to the Red Sea, head around the Horn of Africa, and continue down the eastern seaboard of Somalia to our next destination . . ."

Twenty-four explorers leaned forward in their seats.

"Tanzania!"

The place erupted.

"I bet we're gonna climb Mount Kilimanjaro," said Sailor.

Bryndis gasped. "I've always wanted to see the Serengeti."

Cruz and Emmett turned to each other. "Wildebeests!" they shouted, remembering the stampede of holographic animals that had scared them half to death at orientation.

The holo-map vanished and was replaced by a photograph. It was a weird-looking animal—sort of a cross between an armadillo and an oversize pine cone. Slightly bigger than a cat, it had a cone-shaped head, a pointed snout, and tiny, dark eyes. Large, overlapping, platelike brown scales covered its entire body, stretching all the way to the end of a long flat tail. The creature was licking ants off a tree stump right below the camera with a thin pink tongue that had to be a foot long!

"It's a pangolin," sang Kwento.

"That's right," said Professor Gabriel. "Although it eats ants and termites, it's not part of the anteater family. Nor is it a reptile. It is a mammal—the only known mammal to have such protective scales." Their instructor turned to look at the pangolin. "This fella snapped his own photo while eating dinner. Not a bad selfie, huh? Science has been able to learn a great deal about wildlife through the photos and videos captured by what is known as camera trap technology. Surveillance like this can show us everything from animal behavior to migration patterns to the types of species that inhabit a particular area. Sometimes, researchers discover an animal living in an area that they didn't expect to see there. They may even identify new species!

"Camera traps typically rely on motion or infrared sensors," Professor Gabriel continued, as the lights came up. "They work well but aren't without their issues. The cameras are fixed, so they can only take photos and videos of what occurs directly in front of them. A camera may snap a picture too late, it may not properly adjust for the light level, or the autofocus isn't quick enough to get a good photo. Weather extremes can cause them to malfunction. Plus, the cameras need to be placed in locations where researchers can easily access them to charge batteries and do maintenance. Fortunately, many of these problems have been solved with new technology. Dr. Vanderwick?"

The tech lab assistant director stepped up to the box, unfolded the flaps, and took out what looked like a clear, circular waffle. She placed it on the table. Reaching back into the box, Dr. Vanderwick brought out a handheld remote.

Cruz's shoulders sagged. He'd hoped for something more exciting. Emmett's expression told Cruz he felt the same way. Professor Gabriel was looking around, reading their faces. "Hold on," he cautioned. "We're just getting started."

Dr. Vanderwick punched a few buttons on the remote and the jellylike waffle turned hunter green. It began to stretch and grow and ripple, like some kind of alien slime.

All right! This was *much* better!

In minutes, the waffle had transformed into a group of flat, circular, ridged disks.

"What's it doing?" called Weatherly from the back of the room.

"It's growing leaves," answered Felipe, who was in the front row.

From between the velvety leaves sprouted a dozen or so tiny pinkish red stems. The

stems grew a few inches, curling up to reveal oval blossom heads. It was like watching a nature video in time-lapse, except this was real! Dozens of petals burst open, blossoming into clusters of purple flowers with golden centers.

"African violets!" cried Bryndis.

"They aren't real flowers, of course," Dr. Vanderwick said. "This is a SHOT-bot. It stands for Soft Heliomorphic Observational Traveling robot." Sliding her palm under the plant, the scientist made her way toward the explorers so they could get a closer look. "Dozens of micro solar-powered motors inside the soft silicon shell allow us to program the bot to mimic most any plant, from cactus to cattail. The device is impervious to extreme hot and cold, water, disease, insect invasion, and most animal attacks. Inside the casing is a state-of-the-art camera that can relay images or videos to researchers at a distant base station within seconds."

"Imagine how much we could learn if we were able to follow a pangolin for months, or even years," said Professor Gabriel.

"Rows of lubricated feet allow the SHOT-bot to move in rhythmic waves, or locomotion, much the way a slug travels." Dr. Vanderwick tipped the violets to show them the small lines of suction-cup-like rings. "It can go most anywhere—up steep mountains, through a sandy desert, or even underwater. Also, all maintenance can be done remotely, allowing it to go to the most isolated and extreme regions on Earth, like Antarctica or the Sahara."

Dugan's hand went up. "What if an animal tries to eat it?"

"Sad to say, we did lose a few early prototypes to some hungry critters," said Dr. Vanderwick. "Now we replicate a toxic plant native to the area so animals will avoid it."

Professor Gabriel rubbed his hands together. "Explorers, here is where you come in. Once we reach the port of Mombasa, Kenya, we will help deploy the first wave of SHOT-bots in Tanzania's Serengeti plains in a mission we are calling Operation Animal Selfies."

A dozen hands shot up. Everyone had questions.

"We'll have plenty of time to go over the details," assured their professor. "For now, I want you to understand what is at stake. Along with being the only mammal to have protective scales, the pangolin has another distinction—a tragic one, I'm afraid. It's the most illegally trafficked mammal on Earth. Every year, tens of thousands of these nocturnal animals are poached from Africa and Asia. Pangolins are killed for their meat and beautiful scales, which are used in fashion and traditional medicines in some places in the world. Some people believe the scales can cure everything from asthma to cancer, although science has disproved this time and time again. The scales are made from keratin—the same material that makes up our hair and nails—that's all." Professor Gabriel stepped toward them, intertwining his fingers and shaking his clasped hands the way he often did when he had something important to say. "Pangolins don't do well in captivity, so if we can't save them in the wild, if we can't slow or stop the illegal trade, we will lose these unique creatures."

The lights went down again, and they watched a short holo-video about pangolin poaching. The reporter said that over a million pangolins were killed every year for their meat and scales—making up as much as 20 percent of the illegal wildlife trade. The explorers watched authorities in Asia seize thousands of dead pangolins kept in a filthy storage shed. Each animal had rolled itself into a ball, a position they got into when they were scared or trying to protect themselves. It was heartbreaking.

Feeling his belly tighten, Cruz noticed that Ali, Bryndis, and some of his other classmates had turned away. Cruz was tempted to do the same, but he didn't. If you refused to look, it was easy to pretend it wasn't happening. Still, Cruz was glad when the video was over.

For a moment after the report finished, no one spoke. It was a lot to take in.

"For your next assignment, I want you to create a conservation plan for an endangered African animal," said their teacher. "Consider the issues you will need to address, such as poaching, habitat loss, climate change, or a food source problem. What about society's attitudes and traditions? Choose three major threats, then explore how you'd work to overcome these problems. Who knows? Maybe one of you will come up with a way to help save an animal at risk. You'll find complete instructions on the class website..."

A red bee had popped up in the lower corner of Cruz's tablet—an alert from Mell! She had captured new video near the mystery door on B deck. Unfortunately, Professor Gabriel was looking in Cruz's direction. He would have to wait to view it.

After class, Cruz lagged behind the rest of the explorers filing out. They had a 10-minute break before second period. Once everyone had left, Cruz tapped the message icon on his tablet. He expected to see Jericho Miles. However, Mell had captured video of someone else. The dark-haired woman looked a few years younger than Aunt Marisol. Straight black hair was pulled back with a pearl barrette, revealing two gold hoop earrings. She wore a light-pink shirt under a darker pink cardigan with jeans and tennis shoes. No badge. No lab coat.

The woman wasn't his only problem. Mell's most recent diagnostic test showed that Mell's right forewing was malfunctioning. Cruz typed a message, asking Mell if she thought she could make it back to his cabin safely on three wings. When she responded *affirmative*, Cruz tapped his honeycomb remote pin. "Mell, return to cabin 202. Fly to my desk, then shut off." Hitting the live button on his tablet screen, he watched the world through the rounded lenses of the drone's eyes as she zipped through the tight maze of passages and up two decks. Not until she had swooped under the door of his cabin and landed on his desk did he exhale.

"Hey!" Emmett had stuck his head back in Manatee classroom. "You coming?"

Cruz crooked a finger at his friend. "Mell's got fresh video of the mystery door."

"Oh yeah? Jericho again?" Emmett came toward him.

"Not this time." Slanting his tablet toward Emmett, he played the video. "Ever seen her?"

Studying it, Emmett clicked his tongue. "Nope. Sorry. I got nothing."

Cruz told himself to stay calm. But it was impossible. His heart was racing. His brain was reeling. In those few seconds that Emmett had denied knowing the woman in Mell's video, his glasses had transformed into bright white trapezoids with purple streaks. Cruz had known his friend long enough to decode the morphing frames: white stood for shock or surprise, purple was the color of caution and suspicion, and a trapezoid showed up only when Emmett was nervous. It was a combination Cruz had never before seen in the emotive frames, maybe because his roommate had never lied to him. Until now. The emoto-glasses had betrayed their creator. Emmett *did* know the woman in the video.

Cruz was certain of it.

6

▶ **"ARGGGH!"** Cruz dropped the tiny screw-
driver. It hit the sapphire granite desk with a clink, then rolled onto
the floor.

Kneeling next to Cruz, Emmett placed his chin on the blue granite to
come eye level with the drone. "Congrats, you snapped Mell's wing clean
in half."

Cruz had used too much pressure tightening it. "Can *you* fix her?"

"This wing is a goner, but—"

"Great." Cruz shoved his chair back, nearly tipping over.

"You've been in a crummy mood all day," said Emmett. "It's the
cryptogram, isn't it?"

It had been almost three days, and Cruz was no closer to decoding his mom's cipher. "This could be it, Emmett," he moaned. "This could be the one I can't solve."

"You know what your problem is?"

"Other than I have a busted drone, a ton of homework, and a roommate that keeps pointing out all my problems?"

"If you'd have let me finish, I was going to say we could build her a new wing."

"We could?"

"Not 'we' as in you and me. I meant 'we' as in Fanchon."

Orion's science tech lab chief *did* have the skills, tools, and materials to fix Mell.

"Good idea." Cruz pedaled his chair back to his desk. With his right hand, he scooted Mell into his left palm. Emmett carefully dropped the piece of wing in there, too. Cruz started for the door, then stopped. Should he wait? He had 30 pages of assigned reading for Professor Ishikawa's lecture on the food chain, a quiz tomorrow in Aunt Marisol's class on geologic time eras, and he hadn't even begun Professor Gabriel's conservation assignment. Cruz looked down at the damaged bee in his hand. Mell's golden eyes were dark, her body limp. He couldn't leave her this way. He curled his fingers around the drone. "I'll drop her off and come right back."

"Uh-huh," said Emmett absently. He was already back at his desk.

Cruz met Lani halfway up the grand staircase in the atrium.

"Where are you going?" she asked.

"To the tech lab to see Fanchon. It's Mell..." He opened his fist.

"Oh no! Can I come? I want to meet Fanchon."

"Sure." He led the way up the one and a half flights to the fourth deck.

Waving his OS band in front of the tech lab's security camera, Cruz motioned for Lani to go in ahead of him. He knew she would be as amazed as he'd been the first time he'd laid eyes on the labyrinth of cubicles, bubbling beakers, neon tubes, and other extraordinary experiments.

"Whoa!" Lani's face glowed green under the lights.

"Hello?" called Cruz. "Fanchon? Dr. Vanderwick?"

While they waited for one of the scientists to appear, Lani poked her head into the various nooks. Cruz stayed close. Lani was as curious as he was—sometimes more—which could spell disaster in a place like this.

"Watch it!" warned Cruz. Lani was leaning over a wicker basket containing what appeared to be blueberry muffins. "I've learned that around here, the cuter it looks, the more dangerous it is."

"Achoo!"

Cruz realized the sneeze hadn't come from his best friend. He craned his neck. "Fanchon?"

"There!" Lani pointed to a flash of white moving through the maze of cubicles.

"It's Dr. Vanderwick," said Cruz. "Come on."

They took off after her. She was really moving, darting through the narrow aisles between the partitions. Fortunately, she hadn't buttoned her white lab coat, and it flew out behind her—a perfect flag for them to follow.

Hearing voices, Cruz pulled up. Maybe they shouldn't barge in. "Let's wait until they're done," he whispered to Lani, who nodded.

"...the illness is spreading," a man was saying. Cruz did not recognize the voice. "We're concerned about bronchopneumonia. We have a sick baby now, too."

"I'm so sorry, Moses," said a voice Cruz *did* know. It belonged to Professor Ishikawa. "We do have some good news."

"We've isolated the pathogen," Fanchon chimed in. "It's a mutated strain of a flu virus that's common among humans but has only been seen once before in mountain gorillas."

Cruz and Lani swung to face each other. Mountain gorillas?

Pointing up, Cruz went on his toes so he could peer over the top of the cubicle. Lani did the same, though she could barely get her chin over the partition. Fanchon, Professor Ishikawa, and Dr. Vanderwick had their backs to them. The three adults were facing a computer. On-screen was a young African man in a button-down khaki shirt, the sleeves pushed up to his elbows.

"It's passed from person to animal in the air or by touching a contaminated surface," Fanchon was saying. "A tourist, villager, park ranger—anyone could have exposed them. I'm afraid this strain is more virulent than the one in the previous outbreak. I know I don't need to tell you that a respiratory illness can produce a far worse reaction in gorillas than in humans."

"No, you don't." He rubbed his chin.

"Now for the good news," said Fanchon. "We—Sidril, our team of scientists, and myself—we've developed an antiviral to combat it."

"That *is* good news," said Moses.

"Is remote injection the best way to deliver the medication?" asked Professor Ishikawa.

"For the first group that was infected—yes," answered Moses. "They are used to the tourists and my research and veterinary team. We've used medicated darts before to deliver antibiotics. But the other group will be a challenge. They've had only limited human contact. They're not fully habituated. It would be difficult to get within range. We might be able to dart one, but it would alert the rest and they'd take off."

"We could put the meds in food, say fruit or bamboo shoots," said Dr. Vanderwick.

Fanchon put a hand to her tiger-print head scarf. "How about a mist for them to inhale?"

"The key is going to be getting close enough to make sure every gorilla in the group is treated," said Moses. "*Anything* we try is likely to spook them."

Cruz nudged Lani. "Not if they don't know you're there," he whispered.

Lani giggled. "What do you suggest, wearing a gorilla suit?"

"No. I've got a better idea."

Her smile faded when she saw he was serious. "Well, tell *them*."

Should he interrupt? They were listening to a private conversation, after all. Besides, Fanchon had probably already thought of his plan, along with a million reasons why it wouldn't work.

Lani was tugging on his sleeve. "What are you waiting for?" she hissed. "Spill it!"

There was a chance, a teeny-tiny chance, that Fanchon hadn't thought of it.

"Okay, okay." Going up on his toes, Cruz cleared his throat. Professor Ishikawa, Dr. Vanderwick, and Fanchon turned.

"Cruz?" Professor Ishikawa frowned. "Lani?"

"Sorry," said Cruz. "We didn't mean to eavesdrop. We were looking for Fanchon and happened to overhear." He put a hand to his chest. "Anyway, I was thinking the explorers could do it—get close enough to give the gorillas the medicine, I mean."

Fanchon was giving him a coy grin. She knew what he was going to say.

Cruz swallowed hard. "Do you think...?"

She nodded.

"Can I show...?"

Fanchon was still nodding.

Cruz flew around the side of the partition, put a hand to his shadow badge, and tapped it twice. He caught a whiff of passion fruit, which confirmed Emmett's Lumagine had been activated. Closing his eyes, Cruz imagined a foggy, damp forest high in the mountains, a place where thick green curtains of moss hung from a canopy of gnarled trees and the ground was covered in thick broadleaf plants and ferns. Cruz hoped his vision was close to reality. He'd only seen pictures of the cloud forests in East Africa—the only region on Earth where mountain gorillas are found.

Hearing Lani gasp, Cruz opened his eyes. It had worked! The color of his uniform had turned from its usual stone gray to a vivid green rainforest print.

"Our shadow badges!" Lani was beside him.

"It might work. *Might*," said Dr. Vanderwick. She blew her nose.

"We'll need to add a full face hood and special mask to the uniforms,"

said Fanchon. "Also, we'll have to devise a rainforest fragrance to neutralize the human scent..."

"Then we can go?" pressed Cruz. "You'll let the explorers help with the mission?"

"I'm not your instructor," said Fanchon. "Permission isn't mine to give."

Lani and Cruz turned to their professor with pleading looks.

"We don't usually attempt something so risky with first-year recruits," said Professor Ishikawa, clasping his hands the way he often did in class when he was considering something. "However, there are no other Explorer Academy ships in the area. Given the nature of the emergency, it's likely the faculty would support the mission, though I would have to get their approval, as well as your adviser's."

Only when Lani let out a tiny cry did Cruz realize he was tightly clutching her upper arm with both hands. He let go.

His internal debate finished, Professor Ishikawa straightened. "All right. It's worth a try. But we'll have to act quickly."

Cruz had no sooner gotten back to his cabin than Taryn's voice came over his comm pin. "Attention, all explorers, please check your tablets for an important message."

> *Dear Explorer,*
> *Your help is urgently needed. The explorers have been asked to aid in giving medication to ill mountain gorillas. This mission will be difficult and dangerous, so participation is voluntary. To learn more, please report to the mini CAVE immediately. One explorer from each team will be selected for the expedition unit (unless all members from the same team decline to go).*
> *Fortes fortuna adiuvat,*
> *Professor C. Ishikawa*

Emmett and Cruz hurried to join the explorers filling the passage. Near the entrance to the CAVE, they met up with Lani, Bryndis, and Sailor. The only member missing from Team Cousteau was Dugan.

"It doesn't say here *how* they are going to choose who goes." Sailor tapped a cotton-candy-pink nail against her tablet screen. "I wonder if it will be a competition?"

"I really want to go," said Bryndis. "I chose the mountain gorilla for our conservation assignment. They are my favorite animal. It would be amazing to see them in person."

"If we get to vote," Cruz whispered in her ear, "I'll vote for you."

The smile she gave him made his heart flip.

The CAVE door was opening.

Emmett lifted his chin. "Dugan's not here."

"I know," said Cruz.

"It's not like him to miss this."

"I *know*."

"I mean, the guy is super competitive, there's no way he wouldn't—"

Cruz groaned. Why was it always up to him to rescue Dugan? Cruz punched his comm pin. "Cruz Coronado to Dugan Marsh."

"Marsh here."

"Did you get Professor Ishikawa's message? You coming to the CAVE?"

"No."

"No, you didn't get it, or no, you aren't coming?"

"Yes, I got it. No, I'm not coming."

"Dugan, are you sure? I mean, it's mountain gorillas and a daring mission—"

"I said I'm *not* coming. Marsh, out."

Cruz shook his head at Emmett, who sighed as if to say, "Hey, you tried."

Entering the large oval compartment that was home to the mini CAVE, the explorers were in near-complete darkness. A large spotlight near the center of the chamber illuminated Professor Ishikawa and Monsieur Legrand.

"Good evening, explorers!" Professor Ishikawa's voice echoed through the empty room. "Please place all tablets, phones, and electronic devices near the CAVE entrance."

Ordinarily, that order would include Mell, too, but since she was broken, Cruz figured it was okay to leave her in his pocket. In all the excitement, Cruz had never gotten the chance to ask Fanchon about repairing his drone. He patted his pocket. "Don't worry, Mell," he muttered. "I won't forget."

"Gather round, please," said Professor Ishikawa. "Our mission is to deliver medication to treat and prevent a virus that is spreading through the mountain gorilla population in Bwindi Impenetrable Forest in Uganda. However, there is only room for four explorers on the helicopter. Following this meeting, Monsieur Legrand and I will prepare the mission team for the expedition, but I must tell you, this will not be an easy task. Your trek will take you deep into the jungle. Although we are taking every precaution and mountain gorillas are typically shy animals, they *are* wildlife and can become aggressive if they feel threatened. Also, the park is a protected area, but that doesn't mean poachers or criminals don't cross into it. Now that you know the risks, anyone who would like to opt out of consideration is welcome to do so. No one will think less of you. This is not a classroom project. This is a personal choice." He turned his back to them and began speaking in hushed tones to Monsieur Legrand.

Their teacher was giving them time so that anyone who wanted to quietly slip out of the CAVE could do so. Cruz had no intention of leaving. He glanced at his teammates. Each one returned his determined stare and remained rooted where they were. No one from Team Cousteau was going anywhere. Apparently, neither was anyone else.

Turning back around, Professor Ishikawa seemed pleased to see that all the explorers had stayed. "All right, then," he said. "To get on the mission team, you must earn your place."

The lights in the CAVE came up. A few feet in from the curved black walls, a large circle of hovering disks appeared: six red, then six blue, six green, and, finally, five purple disks. Floating a few inches above the floor, each disk was about two feet in diameter. "Team Magellan, you are assigned the red disks," said Monsieur Legrand. "Team Galileo, you are blue. Team Earhart, you'll be green. Team Cousteau, purple."

"What do we do with them?" asked Femi.

"Stand on them," answered their instructor.

Everyone laughed, until they realized Monsieur Legrand was serious.

Cruz gingerly placed a foot on a purple disk. When it didn't sink, flip, or try to toss him off, he stepped up and put his full weight on it. It was a strange feeling, being off the ground. Bryndis had taken the disk to his right. Lani was on his other side; she was bent down, peeking under her disk—trying to figure out how it worked, no doubt. Cruz noticed a row of 10 square white lights on the floor in front of his disk. They made a straight dotted line leading to Professor Ishikawa and Monsieur Legrand's spotlight in the center of the CAVE. Everyone else had lighted paths, too. The whole floor looked like a giant pizza cut into 23 wedges. Even the ring of colored disks reminded Cruz of pepperoni slices.

"*Attention, s'il vous plaît!*" called Monsieur Legrand. "Settle, stand tall, face me."

Seconds later, a white screen and keyboard materialized in front of each explorer.

"This game will test your knowledge of mountain gorillas," said Professor Ishikawa. "A question will come up on your computer screen. You have thirty seconds to type in your answer. Get it right and your disk moves one light closer to my center circle. Get it wrong or fail to answer in the allotted time, and you'll be eliminated. Your lighted path will go out and your disk will land. If you are knocked out, please quietly remain where you land until the game has ended. The faster you answer, the faster a new question will appear. The first member of each team to make it inside the circle with me will win a spot on the mission team. As usual, we are on the honor system, so please keep your eyes on your own screen and work individually."

Monsieur Legrand held up his hand. "Get ready, explorers."

Cruz placed his hands on the middle row of his keyboard.

"The first question will appear in three ... two ... one ..."

Cruz's eyes raced over the screen: *Name one of the three countries in the world where mountain gorillas are found.* Talk about an easy one! Professor Ishikawa had given them the answer barely an hour ago. A 30-second clock appeared in the corner of his screen and began counting down. Cruz typed: *Uganda.*

Correct!

His disk glided forward. The moment it stopped, a new question appeared: *A typical group of mountain gorillas includes a dominant male that makes decisions and protects the group. What is this leader called?*

Oh, oh! Cruz knew this. It was on the tip of his tongue. What was it? With 10 seconds to go, he remembered and typed in his answer: *silverback.*

Correct!

That was close! His disk moved to the next light.

True or false? The wrinkles around a gorilla's nose, called noseprints, are unique to each animal, the same way human fingerprints are unique to each person.

Cruz was pretty sure the answer was *true.* His fingers flew over the top row of keys.

Correct!

As his purple disk inched closer to Professor Ishikawa, an odd feeling came over Cruz. It felt as if he'd played this game before. But he hadn't, of course. Why was it so familiar?

Bryndis was two lights beyond him. Emmett was one light ahead. Lani and Sailor were neck and neck with him. Another question was on the screen: *How often does a gorilla make a new nest for sleeping?*

Cruz had no clue. He hoped the answer would come to him before he had to make a guess. Within seconds, it did. However, what popped into his head had nothing to do with the question in front of him. Staring down at his hands poised above the keyboard, it hit him. Cruz knew how to decode his mother's message!

7

► *TIME EXPIRED!*

Answer: A gorilla makes a new sleeping nest every night.

The path of lights beneath Cruz's disk went dark. A second later, his computer screen and keyboard vanished. His purple disk sank slowly to the floor. Cruz was out of the game. But that was all right, because now Cruz knew what the dancing boxes in his mother's clue meant—or he would know, as soon as he could get to his tablet.

How could he have been so blind? The cryptogram was based on the alphabet, but they had been using the wrong cipher! And his mom *was* right. He had seen it thousands of times, including tonight. It took all of Cruz's willpower to follow his teacher's instructions and stay on his disk. His tablet was less than 20 feet away, piled with the other electronics next to the CAVE door. Up ahead, Bryndis's disk was crossing into the center circle. She had won! Spinning left and right to see where her teammates were in the game, Bryndis threw her fists up in victory. Cruz smiled. Soon, four explorers stood in the center light with Professor Ishikawa and Monsieur Legrand. The game was over.

"Excellent work!" said the professor. "Please congratulate our winners: Bryndis from Team Cousteau, Felipe from Team Galileo, Shristine from Team Earhart, and Ali representing Team Magellan."

All of the explorers applauded the winners.

"If the mission team will please remain," instructed Professor

Ishikawa, "the rest of you may head topside. Classes are postponed until we return, although—"

Another round of applause—this one twice as loud as the first.

Their instructor held up a hand and they quieted down. "As I was about to say, even though you will not have school, you *will* have a job to do. The rest of you will be mission support staff. You'll be monitoring the technology we'll be using in the field, including our shadow badges, OS bands, and the insect drones Fanchon will be deploying to locate the gorillas. Please report to the conference room tomorrow morning at nine a.m., and Professors Gabriel, Coronado, and Benedict will brief you on your part of the mission."

Before leaving, Sailor, Emmett, and Cruz went to congratulate Bryndis. She hugged each of them in turn. Cruz went last. He couldn't help noticing she held on to him a few seconds longer than everyone else.

"Be careful," Cruz said to Bryndis as he stepped back.

"I will." Bryndis seemed like she wanted to say something else but, with a glance to Sailor and Emmett, changed her mind.

With one last good-luck wave to Bryndis, the four members of Team Cousteau collected their gear and headed out of the CAVE.

In the corridor, Cruz pulled his friends aside. "Our cabin in ten minutes," he whispered. "Come one at a time so nobody gets suspicious."

"What's going on?" asked Sailor.

Cruz waited until Tao and Yulia went by. "Just be there."

Lani nudged Sailor. "He's figured it out." Cruz never could hide anything from Lani.

"You have?" gasped Sailor. "Really?"

Cruz gave her a mysterious smirk. "Ten minutes."

The second the door to cabin 202 shut, Emmett pounced. "What does the message say?"

"Don't know yet," laughed Cruz. "I have to decode it, but now I know *how.*"

Emmett's glasses were yellow-and-pink-striped wheels. "How do you know how?"

"When we were playing the trivia game, this weird feeling came over me. The moving disks, the lighted path—everything in the CAVE felt familiar, but I couldn't put my finger on it. Then I started to type in an answer to one of the questions, and that's when I realized—"

Cruz's tablet chimed. His father was calling. Cruz held up a finger to tell Emmett he would finish their conversation in a minute. Sitting on the edge of his bed, he tapped the screen. "Hey, Dad."

"Hi, son." He was holding his favorite coffee cup, one that Cruz had given him a few years ago for Father's Day. Cruz had decorated it himself, painting a phrase on the side: *Goofy Foot Dad*. Like Cruz, his dad was a goofy foot surfer, which is how their surf shop got its name. "What's new?"

"Lani!" cried Cruz. "Dad, she's here. On *Orion*. With me. She's an explorer now!"

His dad chuckled. "I heard."

"She was an alternate. All this time she was an Explorer Academy alternate, and we never knew!"

"I thought that might make your week."

"Week? Try my whole year. She's on my team, too. She's on Team Cousteau."

"Even better." His dad leaned in. "Listen, I don't have long. Are you free to talk?"

"Yeah. It's just Emmett and me. Lani and Sailor are due any minute. What's up?"

"The police caught another one of the kidnappers."

"But there were three, right?"

"Yep, the ringleader is still on the run. If Tom London—not that that's his real name—is as smart as he seemed, I'm sure those cowboy boots of his are no longer in the state of Hawaii."

"C-cowboy boots?" sputtered Cruz.

"Yeah, he wore a pair of snakeskin-print boots. Ugliest darn things. I gave the police as many details as I could remember about the guy— tall, stubbled chin, good-looking, and those ridiculous boots."

Tom London. So that was his name. Or not. Cruz knew the man in the cowboy boots worked for Nebula, so his dad's news hadn't come as a complete shock. Yet, the fact that Nebula had sent the same man who'd tried to kill Cruz to kidnap his father seemed to make everything so much more . . .

Terrifying.

His mother had been right. The words she'd spoken from her holo-journal were burned into his brain: *Nebula may try to stop you, even hurt you.* Cruz knew Nebula would never give up. They were out there. Somewhere. Waiting to strike.

". . . I doubt Nebula would dare try to kidnap me again," his dad was saying, "but in case they do, I've added some security here as well as downstairs in the store."

"Good," said Cruz. That made him feel better.

There was a soft knock at the door. Emmett went to open it.

Cruz turned his tablet so his father could see Sailor and Lani. "They're here, Dad."

"Hi, girls," said Cruz's dad.

They said their hellos and waved.

"They're here to work on Mom's fourth clue," explained Cruz.

"How's it going?"

"I think I figured it out." Cruz motioned for his teammates to sit beside him. "Dad, I'm sending you a video I took of the cryptogram. Take a look at it."

"Okay."

A minute later, Cruz heard chirping and knew his father was watching it. "See the numbers in the boxes?" Cruz directed his father. "At first, we thought each number stood for a letter of the alphabet—you know, A was one, B was two, and so on. But when we decoded it, the message made no sense. But I got to thinking, what if we had the wrong cipher?

What if the boxes were meant to represent something else—something with twenty-six letters divided into three rows the way the boxes are in the clue? And what if that something had similar-looking boxes that moved? That's when it hit me. The boxes are actually—"

"Keys!" yelled Sailor, bouncing so hard she flung herself off the bed. Blue, pink, and red painted fingers clawed to pull herself back up. Sailor's head popped above the mattress. "They're QWERTY keyboard keys."

"Yes!" crowed Cruz.

"I can't believe I missed it," said Emmett, planting a palm on his forehead. "The boxes even look a little like keys."

Lani tipped her head. "So what does the message say?"

"I was about to decode it," said Cruz.

"Here, we can use my keyboard," said Sailor, placing her tablet beside Cruz's on the bed. "Cruz, play your video. I'll transpose the letters."

"And I'll type them into my tablet and decode the message," finished Lani.

"Be sure to follow the clue exactly the way the boxes move," reminded Emmett.

"Right." Cruz hit play on his tablet. "The first box is red twenty-five."

"The twenty-fifth key is an *N*," said Sailor.

Lani tapped her screen.

"Second box is a green eight."

"That's an *I*," said Sailor.

"Purple eleven," called Cruz.

"*A.*"

"Yellow twenty-six."

Sailor grinned. "That's an easy one: *M.*"

Cruz watched the orange box glide forward. "Orange eleven."

"*A.*"

"Light blue twenty-four."

"*B.*"

"Dark blue eight."

"*I,*" announced Sailor.

They were done.

All eyes turned to Lani, who announced the result: "N-I-A-M-A-B-I."

"Niamabi?" Sailor made a face. "Is that a fish?"

"Could be a person," said Cruz. "Nia Mabi?"

"Mabi, maybe not," joked Lani.

"Might be a place," said Emmett, his fingers flying over his screen. "NI is the internet code for Nicaragua … NI could mean Northern Ireland …"

"Or the North Island of New Zealand," said Sailor. "I'm from the South Island. Wouldn't that be something if we found a piece of the cipher in New Zealand?"

"If it takes us there, you can lead the way," said Cruz.

"Maybe it's a formula," said Lani. She was searching on her tablet, too. "I've got the periodic table. Ni is the chemical symbol for nickel. Am is americium. Bi is … let's see … bismuth. That leaves Ma, which is … nothing."

"Americium *is* radioactive, so I wouldn't try that formula," warned Emmett.

Cruz wasn't coming up with anything either. He sighed. "I guess I was wrong about the whole keyboard thing."

"I wouldn't be so quick to give up," said Lani. "I think we're on the right trail."

"I think so, too," said Sailor. "This new decoding has vowels."

"What about the colors?" interjected Cruz's dad.

Everyone looked at everyone else. Cruz shrugged. "We don't know what those mean, if anything."

"They must stand for something. Otherwise all the numbers would be the same color, right?"

His dad had a point. A message they didn't understand delivered by colorful moving boxes they couldn't interpret. Not exactly progress.

"I've got to get downstairs to open the shop," said Cruz's dad. There was a 12-hour time difference between Egypt and Hawaii. As Cruz was ending his day, his father was beginning his. "Hang in there, guys. You'll solve it. Love you, son."

"Love you, too."

The video window closed.

The lights flickered. Bedtime.

"At least we don't have to get up early for class tomorrow," said Emmett after the girls left. "We can sleep in—lucky us."

"Yeah, lucky us," echoed Cruz, but with an unsolved puzzle, he had a feeling that this was going to be another sleepless night.

A **BELL WAS JINGLING.**
Cruz opened his eyes. His cabin was dark. He was slumped over, his pillow propped up behind him and something sharp digging into his side. There it was again—the bell. It was coming from his tablet. Untangling himself from his sheets, Cruz found the tablet and hit the icon. Beautiful blue eyes were looking at him.

"Bryndis?" Cruz said, his voice still gravelly from sleep. "What's wrong?"

"Nothing," she whispered. She was holding her tablet beneath her chin, and the light from the screen cast a spooky glow over her face. "Everything's perfect. I just got back from training."

Cruz rubbed his eyes. "What time is it?"

"Um ... almost midnight. Sailor's asleep."

He yawned. "She wasn't the only one."

"Sorry. I need a favor. Can I borrow your duffel bag? The zipper on mine broke. Taryn's ordered me a new one, but it hasn't come yet."

"Sure. Do you want me to bring it to you?"

"I'll come to you. If Taryn hears, I don't want you to get in trouble."

"I don't mind—"

"Be there in a minute. Make that half a minute."

It took her 22 seconds, to be exact. Cruz was waiting, his door open a crack. At night, the only light in the explorers' passage came from antique lanterns. Hanging from wire handles, the old ship lanterns were staggered on opposite walls every 10 feet or so. Cruz watched the tall figure scurry through the shadows. Bryndis was wearing the standard moss green tee and her uniform pants. Instead of shoes, she was wearing a pair of polar bear slippers. The white bears stood out in the dappled light.

"Thanks," she said quietly, taking the bag he held out.

"Are you guys leaving early?"

"Seven."

"You'd better get some sleep."

"I'll try." Dipping her head, she ran a finger over the word *CORONADO* engraved on the small gold rectangular plate on the front of the bag. "Thanks again. Good night."

"Night."

Bryndis turned away.

He started to close the door.

"Cruz?"

He opened it again, his breath catching. "Yeah?"

"I was wondering … what you said about voting for me … you're so smart and everything …" Her eyes met his. "You can tell me the truth."

Cruz wasn't following her. "About …?"

"Did you lose the game on purpose?"

"No! I knew you wanted to go, but I didn't lose so you could."

"I wanted … you know …" She stubbed a toe into the wood floor. "I wanted to be sure I'd won—how do you say it in English—fair and square?"

He held up a hand, as if to swear. "Fair and square."

"Okay. Sorry … I guess I'm kind of nervous about the mission. Monsieur Legrand and Professor Ishikawa threw a ton of stuff at us in training. Even with the Lumagine gear covering us practically from head to toe, we still have to be careful around the gorillas. We have to make sure we don't position ourselves between the family members or get accidentally stepped on or lose our footing—it's a lot to remember." She was clutching the strap of his bag so tightly, her knuckles were turning white. "I don't want to make a mistake."

"You won't." Cruz stepped into the passage. "I meant what I said. I would have voted for you, and not because we're friends. You deserve to go. You're a good problem-solver and calm under pressure. I mean, if you can handle Dugan, what's a few sick mountain gorillas, right?"

A grin tugged at her mouth.

"It's *örlög*," finished Cruz.

"My destiny, *já*."

Cruz found himself looking into her eyes: the palest of blues with a faint touch of gray. He felt cool lips brush his cheek, and then she was scurrying back down the hall in her polar bear slippers.

Under the soft golden glow of the lanterns, the metal zipper pull on his duffel sent back one last starburst of light before being swallowed up in the shadows. Standing in his doorway, it dawned on Cruz that Bryndis could have borrowed Sailor's duffel. It would have been much easier, and Sailor wouldn't have minded. So why hadn't she?

He put a hand to his cheek. Why else?

8

CRUZ HEARD A THUD.

His eyes popped open. The thud had been him, rolling into the wall next to his bed. The wind was snapping against the rim of the porthole, shaking the glass. Going up on his knees on his mattress, Cruz peered out the circular window. *Orion* was rising and falling with the choppy, white-tipped swells of the Red Sea. The early morning sunlight was streaking the sky purple and orange. Sliding back across his bed, Cruz reached for his tablet. It was 22 minutes after six. If he hurried, she might still be at breakfast.

Cruz hopped in the shower, then got dressed quickly and quietly so he didn't wake Emmett. Sliding one arm into his jacket, he tiptoed toward the door.

He reached for the doorknob...

"Fanchon to Cruz Coronado."

Cruz cupped his left hand over his pin. "Cruz here," he replied.

"Sorry to wake you," came the muffled reply.

"I'm up."

"Are you in your room?"

"Yeah. I was about to go up to breakfast."

"Can you come to the lab first?" asked Fanchon. "And bring the device I made for you. You know the one."

Cruz's hand immediately went to his lower-right front pocket, where

71

he always kept his octopod. "On my way."

Cruz zipped down the explorers' passage, up the atrium staircase, and up one more flight to the tech lab on the fourth deck. Pausing inside the lab to catch his breath, he heard noises coming from a nearby cubicle. He poked his head inside. The table was heaped with all kinds of things: scissors, test tubes, beakers, SHOT-bots, mini cams, headsets, and several odd gadgets and electronic devices that he couldn't make heads or tails out of. Fanchon was trying to pack everything into a hard-shelled carry-on-size suitcase with wheels.

"You're never going to fit all that in there," he said.

"'Never' is not in my vocabulary." Fanchon barely looked up, her hands flying as she packed supplies. She was moving so quickly, the ladybugs on her white apron were a blur. A matching head scarf covered her mass of caramel-colored curls. "We're leaving in a half hour, and as you can see, I'm not quite ready. Sidril's running late, too." She paused from her frenetic packing. "Did you bring the octopod?"

He handed it over.

"Thanks." She saw his worried expression. "I probably won't need it. I'll return it to you as soon as I get back from the mission—unused, I'm sure. I would have made one for myself, but there wasn't time."

Cruz watched her slide the orb into a clear envelope made of bubble wrap. Each of the bubbles was filled with a milky aqua liquid. Fanchon sealed the envelope, rolled the edges in around the ball, and tucked the whole thing into the corner of her case.

Blowing air through her cheeks, Fanchon stepped back. "Okay, I think that's about as much as I can fit in here, don't you?" She shut the lid to the case and snapped the latches. With a grunt, she slid it off the desk and onto the floor. She rolled it to the corner of the cubicle, where another identical case sat.

Flinging her apron over her head, Fanchon rushed out, then reappeared a few minutes later wearing a puffy green parka with a shadow badge on the chest. She had a bulging backpack over one shoulder and her duffel over the other. "Where *is* that assistant of mine?" She tapped her communications pin. "Fanchon to Sidril Vanderwick."

"Sibril here. I know. Coming."

Did she say "Sibril"? Dr. Vanderwick sounded funny. Must be some interference on the comm frequency.

"Hurry," said Fanchon. "We need to get the equipment up to the helicopter pad now."

"I can help," offered Cruz, lifting the thick strap of the duffel from her shoulder and transferring it to his own. He grabbed the handle of one of the black suitcases. "We've got this."

"Thanks, Cruz. Sidril, meet us at the pad."

"Roger."

Fanchon reached for the other case, and they headed for the elevator. Cruz rolled the suitcase into the lift after her, pressing the button for the weather deck. The door closed. As they tipped their heads back to watch the indicator light, Cruz asked a question he might never have dared to ask if they hadn't been alone. "Fanchon, do you think this will work?"

She swished her mouth back and forth. "Honestly? I don't know. A million things could go wrong. On the other hand, if most of it goes right, we'll have saved these animals, and maybe an entire population." Fanchon glanced at him. "Kind of exciting, huh?"

Cruz had to admit it was.

The elevator door opened. Professor Ishikawa, Bryndis, Ali, Felipe, and Shristine were already in the observation roost on *Orion*'s top deck. Cruz had hoped to catch Bryndis's eye, but she was sitting in one of the nubby olive green chairs, her head bent over her tablet. Cruz and Fanchon added their gear to the luggage on the cart near the door that led to the helicopter pad.

"Thanks again," Fanchon said to Cruz, "for *everything*."

"Anytime."

"*Achoo!*" It was Dr. Vanderwick. She was coming through the stairwell door with her duffel. She looked awful. Her nose was red. Her eyes were puffy. And her usually perfect pretzel bun was lopsided, its pearl barrette hanging on the unraveling clump of hair for dear life. "*Achoo! Achoo!*"

"A triple-decker sneeze," said Ali. "Impressive."

"Sidril!" Fanchon hurried to her assistant. "Are you okay?"

"I'm fide. I'm fide," insisted Dr. Vanderwick, her stuffy nose not allowing her to correctly pronounce the word "fine." She tried to wave them away, but everyone could clearly see she was nowhere near "fide."

Fanchon said what they were all thinking. "Sidril, you're sick. You're in no condition to go on this mission."

"But you neeb me. There's so much work. We have to set up the lab and debloy the buttaflies . . . and brebare the mebidcation and . . . and . . . *achoo!*" Dr. Vanderwick pulled a tissue from her pocket. She blew her nose. Her bun fell out. Cruz picked up the pearl barrette that hit the floor and handed it back to her.

"I'll manage," said Fanchon, spinning her toward the elevator and nodding to Felipe to press the button. "What I need is for you to get some rest. If you're feeling better tomorrow, you can head up the support team from here. Go to sick bay."

"But—"

"Sick bay. *Now.*"

"Okay." With one last sniffle, Dr. Vanderwick shuffled onto the elevator.

"I hope we still get to go," Cruz heard Shristine say softly to the other explorers.

"We'll go," said Ali. "We *have* to go. The gorillas are depending on us."

At that, Bryndis's head shot up. "We're not going?" She saw Cruz and sat taller. Having not noticed him when he came in, she was no doubt wondering what he was doing there.

"We're going, all right," Professor Ishikawa said firmly.

Suddenly, they were blasted by a sharp gust of wind. The door to the helicopter pad had opened. "All set?" asked Captain Roxas, their pilot. "I've got to get you to Khartoum by ten."

Fanchon spun toward Cruz. "I'm going to need your help one more time."

"Okay." Cruz went around to the other side of the luggage cart so he could give Captain Roxas a hand wheeling it outside.

Fanchon put a hand on her hip. "Not with that."

"Oh. What, then?"

"The mission."

Cruz's neck swiveled so fast a cramp shot up his head. "The ... the what?"

"Sidril was right. I do need help. How fast can you pack?"

"But I ... I don't know about viruses ... or ... or making medications ... or *anything*."

"You'll learn," she said easily.

Cruz stared at her, dumbfounded. Fanchon *was* serious.

One eyebrow arched to meet her ladybug-print head scarf as she bent forward. "Kind of exciting, huh?"

"**LOOK DOWN, EXPLORERS!**" Professor Ishikawa's voice rang out through the airplane. "That's the Bwindi Impenetrable Forest."

The plane was banking. It gave Cruz a perfect view of the rolling hills so thick with trees he couldn't find a space anywhere.

Bryndis was leaning over to look, too. "That's where we're going? Now I see why they call it impenetrable."

Cruz slipped his mind-control camera down from his head to cover his eyes. He'd been taking photos almost nonstop since they'd left *Orion*—first, in the helicopter as they left the brilliant turquoise waters of the Red Sea behind for the golden dunes and rocky outcrops of the Nubian Desert, and then as they continued their journey south from Khartoum, Sudan, in *Condor,* the Academy's plane. The plane had followed the winding path of the White Nile River into Uganda, over scrublands and savannas, rainforests and foothills. Cruz planned to send a few of his best shots to his dad and his aunt when they landed in Kisoro.

Aunt Marisol!

"Uh-oh," he said.

Bryndis glanced up from her tablet. "What?"

"I never got a chance to tell my aunt I was going on the mission. Everything happened so fast. I had to pack, like, in two minutes." He'd also had to borrow Emmett's duffel, after loaning his to Bryndis.

"I'm sure Emmett or Taryn will let her know."

To be safe, though, he would call when they got on the ground.

Bryndis was tapping her fingers on the armrest between them. Each fingernail was painted a different color. Sailor's handiwork, no doubt.

Bryndis caught Cruz staring. "I know, I know. I'm a regular rainbow, thanks to you-know-who."

Cruz laughed. He knew who. He went back to his view of the mountains.

Rainbow. The word stuck in his brain like a splinter. In her journal, his mom had said something about rainbows.

"I told her my pinkie nail should have been pink, not purple, but you know Sailor..." Bryndis was still talking.

What had his mom said? It took him a few minutes to remember...

By now you've seen it thousands of times. It's as familiar as a rainbow.

Could it be...?

Had she meant...?

Yes! Of course! Cruz bolted upright so fast he kicked the seat in front of him.

"Hey!" yelped Felipe.

"Sorry." Cruz had been on the right track decoding the cryptogram. The thing that he'd seen thousands of times *was* a keyboard. But when his mother had said *It's as familiar as a rainbow,* she wasn't comparing the keyboard to a colorful arch made from water shining through sunlight. No, she was giving him instructions. His mom was telling him to put the colorful boxes in the order they appear in the visible light spectrum, the way you'd see in a rainbow: red, orange, yellow, green, light blue, dark blue, and violet. That had to be it. It couldn't be a coincidence that the moving boxes in the cryptogram were the same seven colors found in every rainbow!

Cruz bent to reach beneath Felipe's seat and with shaky fingers slid open the zipper of his backpack. Cruz took out his tablet. He angled his back toward the plane's window so Bryndis wouldn't peek over his shoulder. He took a long, deep breath before trying once again to decode the message:

Cruz had solved the cryptogram!

He wanted to let out a big "wahoo!" but, naturally, he couldn't. Not here. He could do nothing here, not even text his friends to let them know of his breakthrough. The celebration would have to wait until *Condor* touched down in Kisoro. Namibia was on the west coast of Africa—a couple thousand miles from Uganda. Even so, Cruz was on the right continent and heading in the right direction. That was something. No, that was *everything*. Cruz leaned back in his seat, finally able to close his eyes. The fourth piece of his mother's cipher was hidden somewhere in Namibia.

Cruz's eyelids flew open.

But where?

"DON'T YOU LIKE your rolex?"

Cruz glanced at Bryndis's untouched plate.

By the time they'd reached the gorilla research center on the outskirts of the Bwindi Impenetrable Forest, Cruz had been so hungry he would have eaten a bowl of shredded paper if it had been set in front of him. Instead, Dr. Moses Najjemba, whom Cruz remembered from the video call, his assistant, Jendy Ojara, and a few others on the staff had prepared wraps called rolexes. A traditional round Ugandan flatbread called chapati was fried on top of an egg omelet, then filled with shredded carrots, fresh tomato slices, and cheese before being rolled up. Dr. Najjemba said "rolex" was short for "rolled eggs." Each rolex was served with a bowl of boiled beans on the side. It was simple, warm, and delicious—a perfect meal after a long day of traveling. They also had their choice of mineral water, iced tea, or passion-fruit-orange-pineapple juice. Cruz had chosen juice.

"It's good, but . . ." Bryndis played with a slice of tomato with her fork. "I have a headache."

No wonder. The ride from Kisoro in the four-by-four had been rough. They'd spent the last hour and a half being flung side to side and up and down like ingredients in a tossed salad as the vehicle navigated the bumps, ruts, and potholes along the dirt road.

"You should eat something," said Cruz. "Long day tomorrow."

"I know," said Bryndis. "Fanchon's sending out the insect drone spotters to locate the gorillas in the morning. Depending on where they are, Professor Ishikawa said we could be hiking for hours to reach them."

He nudged the hand holding her fork. "So eat."

"Okay, Dad." She smirked, spearing the tomato.

"Did you hear?" Ali, on Cruz's other side, was elbowing him. "It's against the law for kids our age to trek into the park to see the gorillas. What if they won't let us go?"

Cruz scooped up the last of his rolex. "They'll let us."

"How do you know?"

"We're not kids. We're explorers."

Ali sat up taller. "Yeah. Right."

Sure enough, as they were finishing dessert (warm mango-pear tarts—yum!), Dr. Najjemba explained that while it was illegal for anyone under the age of 15 to go on the gorilla treks for tourists, a special exemption had been made for the explorers of the Academy. "We are grateful for your help," said their host at the head of the table. "We're facing a situation that could get out of hand if we don't act soon."

"Habitat loss, war, hunting, disease—they have reduced the entire population of mountain gorillas to two protected areas in the world," said Professor Ishikawa.

"Half of the gorillas live here in Bwindi, and the other half are found in the three parks in the Virunga Mountains, south of here, that span Uganda, Rwanda, and the Democratic Republic of the Congo," explained Dr. Najjemba. "And an epidemic in any of these areas would be disastrous."

"Mountain gorillas are sensitive to human diseases," said Fanchon, seated at the foot of the table. "Something that seems harmless to us, like the common cold, can kill them."

Now Cruz understood why Fanchon had been so insistent that an ill Dr. Vanderwick stay behind on *Orion*.

"Why don't they keep people out of the parks?" asked Felipe.

"If only it were that simple." Dr. Najjemba placed the fingertips of both hands together to make a tent over his plate. "Unfortunately, the very thing that puts the mountain gorillas at risk is also what is helping to save them. You see, the money earned from ecotourism is used to maintain the parks and protect the gorillas from harm. Precautions are taken, of course, when it comes to visitors. A limited number of permits are issued, and they can only view those gorillas that have become habituated, or used to people. Tourists must wear masks and maintain a distance of at least twenty-five feet from the gorillas. But there are plenty of other ways that the animals can come in contact with us. As you'll see tomorrow when you hike in, the park is surrounded by communities. People have logged the forest right up to the border of the park in order to farm the land. Gorillas sometimes forage in the banana fields. Over the years, we've seen outbreaks of scabies, a skin infestation caused by mites, which can be fatal in gorillas. The animals are exposed to the mites by touching the clothing and blankets that are hung on the wash lines." Dr. Najjemba looked out at the explorers, his eyes narrowing. "So my question for you is, how do we coexist? How do we strike a balance that is healthy for both humans and gorillas?"

Everyone waited for Dr. Najjemba to give them the solution, but he merely reached for his coffee.

After dinner, Jendy showed the explorers where they would be spending the night. Cots had been set up for them in two small rooms at the back of the log building, one for boys and one for girls. In their room, Cruz waited so Felipe and Ali could choose their beds first. He was glad when they left the cot by the window for him. Before getting ready for bed, he sent two texts. The first was to Aunt Marisol to let her know that his mother's clue was sending them to Namibia. She needed to pass the information on to Captain Iskandar, as well as work the destination into their curriculum. The second text went to Lani, Emmett, and Sailor:

Have solved Mom's cryptogram! Will explain when I get back! Love, Cruz
That ought to drive Sailor nuts.

Cruz had barely unzipped his duffel when Fanchon poked her head in the room. She was wearing a watermelon-print head scarf, safety goggles, a pair of latex gloves, and an orange apron with white polka dots that read *Science: Like Magic Only Real!* Fanchon crooked her finger at Cruz. "We have work to do."

So much for getting to bed early.

In the small lab at the other end of the building, Fanchon had already set up her equipment in a corner. She handed Cruz a pair of safety goggles and protective gloves identical to her own. He snapped himself in the face putting on his goggles. *Ouch!* Cruz was nervous—even more nervous than when Fanchon had taught him to use the Universal Cetacean Communicator helmet to talk to the whales. He didn't want to make a mistake.

"I've already loaded the darts for Dr. Najjemba's team, but we need to fill the nebulizers for ours," said Fanchon.

"Nebu-what?"

"Nebulizers. Spray bottles." She pretended to squirt the air. "The explorers are going to spray the antiviral into the air near each gorilla. When the animal takes a breath, he or she will inhale the mist." She had her back to him. "You want to get the nebulizers? They're in the case on the counter. I'll get a tray."

Cruz gently rummaged around until he found a box with about two dozen tiny spray bottles. Each was about the size of a cap to a thick felt-tip pen. Turning, Fanchon placed a clear plastic tray with a grid of holes on the counter next to him. She unscrewed the top from a nebulizer and put its bottom section into one of the holes. Oh, he got it! The tray supported the bottles so you didn't have to hold them in your hands to fill them. Cruz followed her lead—one bottle for each hole. Next, Fanchon brought him a test tube filled with a hazy pink liquid. It reminded him of pink lemonade, but Cruz knew better. "Fill each nebulizer to the inside line, please," she instructed. "While you do that, I'm going to mix up the rainforest scent that will mask the explorers' presence."

Cruz tried to pour slowly so he wouldn't spill the mixture but couldn't keep his hand from trembling. The gloves made his grip feel weird. Cruz's safety glasses were beginning to fog up. He felt a bead of sweat trickle down his temple. This was too much pressure. He couldn't do it...

A hand was on his. "Take your time," said Fanchon. She guided him through filling a few bottles, then lifted her hand away to watch him finish the rest on his own. "Nice work."

"I... I'm sorry, Fanchon." Cruz set the test tube in its holder. "You must have thought I'd be better at this science stuff... you know, 'cause of my mom."

"Cru-uz." Fanchon stretched his name to two syllables. "Nobody is a natural at 'this science stuff,' as you put it. Even when you have a talent or a passion for something you still have to learn the skills. Also, no one expects you to be anything other than yourself—especially not me."

He stared into the pink liquid. "I don't want to disappoint... anybody."

Sliding her goggles up, Fanchon leaned on the counter. "I didn't know your mom, I'm sorry to say, and I don't know your dad, but I *do* know your aunt. And I can tell you that you'd have to work pretty darn hard to let her down. Long before you ever got accepted into the Academy, she'd tell anyone who would listen what a great student you were."

Cruz lifted his eyes. "Really?"

"Sometimes, I'd see the postcards before she sent them to you—you know, the ones you had to decode?" Fanchon chuckled. "She said she had to keep making them more difficult because you were figuring them out so quickly."

Thinking about his aunt, he began to relax.

Fanchon tilted her head. "Now, as for what I think of you ..."

Cruz instantly tensed again.

"If any other explorer had been in the observation deck when Dr. Vanderwick had shown up sick this morning"—Fanchon waved a hand—"I would be standing here alone."

Cruz didn't know whether to believe her, mainly since one of those explorers happened to be his brilliant roommate. But he sure wanted to.

"Which reminds me, since you're here ..." Fanchon reached into the black suitcase and brought out the fluid-filled bubble wrap containing his octopod. Unwrapping the black orb, she held it out. "I believe this belongs to you."

As Cruz slid the octopod back in his pocket, he felt a prick in his palm. *Mell!* Cruz carefully lifted out the tiny bee and her broken wing. Holding the pieces in his outstretched hand, he explained to the tech lab chief that Mell had been the reason he'd gone to *Orion*'s lab, which is how he ended up overhearing her conversation with Dr. Najjemba. "Can you fix her? I ... I mean, will you?"

Taking the drone, she snickered. "Her?"

His face warmed. "That's her name. Mell."

Fanchon's gaze honed in on the honeycomb pin on his jacket. "Is that—"

"A remote for her. Lani made it." Cruz realized his mistake the instant the words were out. Fanchon would want to know how Lani could have possibly made a remote for Mell when she'd only just joined the Academy.

Fanchon was holding the bee up to the light, carefully examining her. Maybe she hadn't heard his slip. "Looks like an Apis 774-A model with a second-gen graphene aerogel body—"

"Does that mean you'll—"

"Give me a couple of days once we get back to the ship. I'll have her as good as new. Better, actually."

He let out a breath. "Thanks, Fanchon."

"In the meantime, let's keep her protected." Opening a drawer,

Fanchon took out a small clear box. Tucking a cotton ball into the bottom of the box, she laid Mell and her broken wing inside, replaced the cover, and rolled the box up in the bubble wrap from the octopod. "All right, tech lab assistant, let's get back to work." Pulling her goggles down, Fanchon moved to her tablet to read off her list. "Okay, where were we? ... Darts. Check. Nebulizers. Check. Rainforest scent. Check. Next, we've got to check the face masks, then run diagnostics on the butterfly drones to make sure their optics and transmitters are functioning properly and sending data back to *Orion*. Also, since we're going to be deploying some SHOT-bots before we leave, we've got to test those, too ..." She glanced up. "Too much? Maybe I should let you get some sleep and finish this myself—"

"I can do it." Cruz felt better now. "I won't let you down, Fanchon."

Brown eyes blinked behind a pair of goggles. "I never doubted it."

THE NEXT MORNING, UNDER A CHALKY SKY that threatened rain, Cruz and the other explorers, along with Professor Ishikawa and Fanchon, set out for the south entrance of Bwindi Impenetrable National Park. Dr. Najjemba's vet team had already left for the day. They were heading for another entrance to the park, where the infected group of habituated gorillas was often seen.

A young Batwa guide named Kuzi led the explorers down the dirt road behind the research center. As they walked between the banana fields, Kuzi told them his ancestors had lived in the area for centuries. He was the first one in his family to go to college. He was studying to be a biologist, specializing in primate research. Marching briskly, Cruz tapped his walking stick out ahead of him. Kuzi had given each of them a thin but sturdy carved wooden stick about shoulder-height. "There are no roads in the park, only trails," he'd said. "Your sticks will help you navigate the mountain paths, which can be very slippery in wet weather."

Bryndis walked beside Cruz. All the explorers were wearing their rain ponchos and wide-brimmed hats, so Cruz couldn't see her face.

"How's your head?" Cruz asked her.

"Okay," she said in that way you do when you really aren't okay but don't want to be quizzed about it.

Maybe Bryndis was coming down with something—Dr. Vanderwick's cold? Their OS bands monitored body temperature, heart rate, respiration rate, blood pressure, even white blood cell count. If Bryndis was getting sick, her band would alert Taryn and the support team back on *Orion*. Since no one had prevented her from going on the mission, Cruz figured Bryndis was tired from traveling. Cruz knew he sure was.

As they neared the park, Cruz saw what Dr. Najjemba had been talking about the night before. You could see a distinct straight boundary line where developers had stopped clear-cutting the trees.

"Look at that!" Shristine pointed to the tree line. "Good thing they created the park."

"Protecting the gorillas is important," said Kuzi. "Yet, the solution came at great cost to my people."

"The Batwa were among the first inhabitants of the region," explained Professor Ishikawa. "They are—were—a hunter-gatherer society. They lived here for centuries, peacefully coexisting with the gorillas. But in the late twentieth century, when the sanctuary was created, the Batwa were evicted from the jungle by the government— some rather violently."

"My great-grandparents and grandparents moved to Kisoro," said Kuzi, "but it was a struggle to survive. Some of the Batwa earned their living by reenacting our ancient hunts and ceremonies for tourists. Others, like my father, became gorilla guides."

"Imagine losing your home, your culture, your traditions—your whole way of life," said Professor Ishikawa.

Cruz remembered last night's discussion at dinner. Now he understood why Dr. Najjemba had not answered the question he had posed to the explorers. Striking a balance between humans and gorillas was a lot more complicated than Cruz had realized.

They'd reached the trailhead. All that marked the entrance was a dingy, bent metal yellow-and-green sign that read: BWINDI IMPENETRABLE NATIONAL PARK. ABSOLUTELY NO ENTRANCE PAST THIS POINT WITHOUT A GUIDE. Inside the entrance, they took a brief break so Fanchon could touch base with the explorers back on *Orion*. The support team was analyzing fresh data from the five butterfly drones Fanchon had deployed at dawn to track the gorillas. While they waited, the team put on their micro communication headsets. The wire-thin earpiece with a microphone attached would allow everyone to communicate using the softest of whispers. Hooking the headset around his ear, Cruz took in his surroundings. On both sides of the worn path, the jungle was so thick with evergreen and deciduous trees, shrubs, vines, and ferns, Cruz could barely see more than a few feet into it.

"I think we've locked on to our gorillas!" Fanchon's voice bubbled with excitement. She huddled with Kuzi to show him the video stream and confirm this was the group they were looking for.

It was time to go.

"According to our drone data, we've got a long hike ahead," explained Professor Ishikawa. "Also, gorillas are nomadic—they travel about a half mile per day— so we may need to make

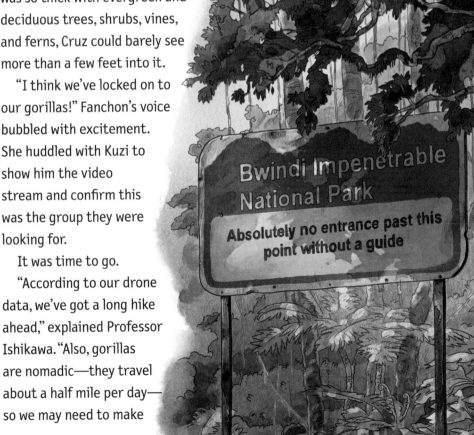

Bwindi Impenetrable
National Park

Absolutely no entrance past this
point without a guide

adjustments as we go. But don't worry, the other explorers on *Orion* are analyzing the tracking data for us. Let's move out. Kuzi and Fanchon will take the lead. I will bring up the rear."

At first, the wide, flat trail allowed them to walk in pairs. However, the path quickly narrowed, the thick brush sweeping their shoulders and ankles. Cruz fell in behind Bryndis. A few miles in, the dense canopy of trees closed in over them. The jungle hid the birds that warbled from high in the branches. Every now and then they'd hear the screech of a monkey, but Cruz didn't see one. The group trekked up and down one steep canyon after another. Kuzi was right. The walking sticks did help you keep your footing on the muddy, rocky slopes.

As they climbed, the giant pines, firs, and mahogany trees gave way to smaller deciduous trees, bamboo, herbs, and ferns. Puffs of fog clouds floated past them like lost ghosts. A light rain began to fall. It tapped out a soft rhythm on Cruz's hat. Summiting yet another hill, the group found themselves in a grassy clearing. Cruz was breathing hard. Glancing past Bryndis, he saw Fanchon's hand in the air—a signal for everyone to stop and remain quiet.

Still huffing, Cruz could feel his heart thumping. Were they going in the wrong direction? Had they lost the gorillas?

For a moment, the only sound was the patter of rain on leaves and ponchos, then came Fanchon's excited hiss in Cruz's ear. "The gorillas are coming this way!"

Cruz's pulse was racing. He could hardly wait to get his first glimpse of the animals.

Turning, Bryndis pushed her hood back, and Cruz's grin quickly vanished. Her face was pasty white, her eyelids heavy. She swayed to one side.

Bryndis was going to pass out!

10

CRUZ CLAMPED a hand on her arm to steady her. "You okay?" he whispered.

"Uh-huh. I just need a minute."

"Maybe we should tell Professor Ishikawa—"

"No, no. I'll be fine. I took some aspirin at our last rest stop. Besides, I'm not about to let a little headache stop me from seeing the gorillas."

Cruz wasn't sure what to do. Should he tell their professor that Bryndis was ill? If she *was* sick, she could expose the gorillas to an infection. On the other hand, if it was only a headache, she'd never forgive him.

Cruz lifted Bryndis's water bottle out of her pack, unscrewed the top, and handed it to her. She gave him an eye roll but drank. A few minutes later, her cheeks had more color and her eyes were brighter.

They were moving again. Kuzi was leading them behind a thicket of bushes near the top of the hill. Cruz kept an eye on how Bryndis was hiking. She didn't stumble. When Professor Ishikawa gave them the signal, Bryndis, Ali, Felipe, and Shristine sprang into action. They flung off their ponchos and rain hats. They removed their comm pins, GPS pins, and all hair clips and jewelry, tucking everything into the pockets of their uniforms. Unzipping their packs, the explorers pulled out their gloves and hoods with oxygen masks. Fanchon had explained to Cruz that the masks would protect the gorillas from being exposed to human germs and bacteria, as well as keep the explorers from inhaling the antiviral. The hoods went over their heads, covering their faces and micro headsets. The explorers worked quickly and efficiently. Monsieur Legrand had trained them well. Once the team was in their gear, the members lined up side by side. Fanchon sprayed the back of each hood with the forest fragrance she'd created to neutralize their scent. Cruz was supposed to follow behind and give out the nebulizers, except he wasn't. He was staring across the meadow, mesmerized by the sight of a dozen dark, furry masses moving smoothly through the wet grasses. He could make out the gorillas' conical black heads and muscular shoulders. Even walking on all fours, they were much larger than he'd expected.

A sharp tug on his sleeve brought him back to reality. Fanchon was frowning at him. With an apologetic nod, Cruz got busy handing out the nebulizers. When he gave Bryndis hers, she gave him a smile—a real smile instead of a forced one. The aspirin must be working.

Fanchon was monitoring the drone video of the gorillas on her tablet. "We have to be sure the group is definitely stopping before we can deploy," she said quietly.

After about 10 minutes, the tech lab chief gave the thumbs-up. Professor Ishikawa motioned for his team to huddle up around Fanchon's tablet. He gave each person specific instructions on which gorillas they were to target. "Remember, do it the way we practiced in the CAVE," he said. "Your nebulizer will not be camouflaged, so keep it hidden in your glove as best you can. Move slowly. Watch for the blue light in the upper-right corner of your face mask. It will go on when you are within three feet of another team member. Watch for that so you don't collide. Radio silence unless it's an emergency. Most important, trust one another. Everyone clear? Good. Let's go."

Cruz felt the sting of envy. He wished he was going, too.

The explorers on the mission team put a hand to their shadow badge and tapped twice. Shristine and Ali closed their eyes. Bryndis and Felipe did not. Cruz would have kept his eyes open, too. Both Emmett and Fanchon had told them that looking at your surroundings was the best way to give the Lumagine bio-net a precise visual to match.

Bryndis clutched the nebulizer to her heart, wrapping her fingers tightly around it. As Cruz watched, the four team members slowly morphed into their cloud forest environment. The transformation was like a slow-rolling wave on the ocean. It started with their heads, then gradually moved down to their shoulders, waists, legs, and, finally, their feet. Now completely camouflaged, the explorers were practically invisible. They blended in so well with the ferns, herbs, and grasses that as Cruz helped Fanchon scoop up their rain gear, he accidentally stepped on someone's foot.

"Cruz!" Shristine yelped.

"Oops! Sorry."

Professor Ishikawa signaled it was time to go, and the explorers headed into the meadow. At least, Cruz assumed they did. He couldn't see anyone, although he did see the grasses part and the indentation of footprints on the wet blades.

Cruz exhaled. His job was done. There was nothing to do now but stay hidden, watch, and wait for the team to return. He pulled the headset from his ear and let it dangle over his shoulder.

Hunkering behind the bushes, Cruz got out his MC camera and trained the zoom lens on the group of gorillas about a hundred yards off. The rain glittered on their furry, powerful bodies. Some of the animals settled under a sheltering fern to doze, while others foraged for food. Cruz watched one gorilla strip the bark off a small tree and eat the bugs inside. She seemed to delight in licking the ants from her fingers. It reminded Cruz of eating fried chicken with his dad. The younger gorillas played, wrestling and tumbling and chasing each other. Cruz took several photos. Panning slowly, Cruz's lens came to rest on a small, fuzzy head. A baby! Two slim, furry arms twined around its mother's neck, as it leaned against her broad shoulder. The adult gorilla cradled her child against her hip, stroking its back. The mother shifted, and Cruz caught a glimpse of frosted fur.

He gasped. "A silverback!"

She was actually a *he*! And he was the leader of this group.

"He is holding his son," whispered Kuzi, startling Cruz. Kuzi had knelt next to Cruz with a set of binoculars. "Silverbacks protect and play with all their children, but they must become the sole caregiver when the mother is no longer around, as in this case."

"No mom?" gulped Cruz. "What happened?"

"She was killed by poachers. The silverback has cared for his child ever since. Other female gorillas will not adopt an orphan, so it's up to the father. He will make sure the child is fed and protected. He'll even bring him in his nest to sleep."

Poor little guy, thought Cruz. *He must miss his mother.*

The infant looked up at his father with innocent brown eyes. A strong arm nestled him closer. The silverback began to groom his son, parting the fur on the small head with his giant, yet gentle, hands. Cruz didn't know a lot about gorillas, but the baby didn't seem as energetic as the other children. His eyes and nose seemed watery, too. Could this be the ill baby Dr. Najjemba had mentioned to Fanchon?

"Is he sick?" asked Cruz.

Kuzi gave a solemn nod.

Cruz hoped they weren't too late.

The silverback patted the baby's back the way a human dad would, and the child drifted off to sleep in his father's arms the way a human child would. It was a bit eerie how alike they were to humans, thought Cruz. He thought he saw the branches of a bush beside the silverback bend, a sign that one of the explorers was nearby spraying the antiviral, but he couldn't be sure.

Cruz didn't know how long he watched the pair, but he was surprised when Fanchon tapped his shoulder. "They're back," she said.

Already?

Ali was tugging off his hood when Cruz reached him. "We did it!"

Professor Ishikawa put a finger to his lips to remind them to keep it down.

Felipe and Shristine were removing their hoods, too. Cruz laughed. With the rest of their uniforms still camouflaged, the trio floated

in front of him, looking like disembodied heads. He looked around for Bryndis's head to appear, too.

"It was awesome," whispered Shristine. "I was so close I could have touched them."

"One almost touched me!" added Felipe. "Did you see how much their fingers look like ours?"

"And their ears and eyes!" gasped Shristine.

"Did you spray the silverback?" asked Cruz. "And his baby?"

"Yes, both," said Shristine proudly, pulling off her gloves. "They were mine."

"Now I get what it must have been like talking to the whales, Cruz," said Ali. "It was the best thing ever!"

"Uh-huh." Cruz was still looking for his teammate. "Uh . . . guys? Where's Bryndis?"

Everyone stopped.

"She's probably still finishing her assignment," said Professor Ishikawa evenly. "Give her a few more minutes."

Their initial enthusiasm evaporating, the explorers turned to face the clearing where the gorillas were still resting, eating, and playing. With his binoculars, Cruz searched the grass for the slightest movement, *anything* that would indicate Bryndis was on her way. "There!" he pointed to the swaying grasses.

"I think that's the wind," said Felipe.

He was right. A light breeze was rippling through the meadow.

A few minutes turned to five. Then ten.

A chill went up Cruz's back. He didn't like this. They should have heard from her by now. As he was about to say that very thing to Professor Ishikawa, their teacher put a hand to his headset. "Base to Bryndis. Come in, Bryndis."

No reply.

Cruz's stomach tightened. "Fanchon, how long will the Lumagine last?"

"She's got several hours before both it and the rainforest scent wear off. She's in no danger of being discovered." Fanchon patted his shoulder.

"She's a smart explorer. I'm sure she'll be fine."

But Cruz wasn't convinced, and Fanchon wouldn't be either if she knew what he knew.

"We should go after her." Felipe reached for his hood.

Shristine and Ali started to do the same.

"Hold on," said Professor Ishikawa. "I've already got one missing explorer. I don't need any more. Besides, how exactly do you plan to find a person that is virtually invisible?"

Mumbling, the three dropped their heads.

"I can try to patch into her OS band to get a fix on her location," suggested Fanchon. "We're in a remote area, though. I may need help from the support team on *Orion* to get a lock."

"Ask for Emmett," said Cruz. "He locked on to my OS band when I was trapped in the cave in Turkey."

"Do it," hissed the professor.

Sinking to her knees, Fanchon set her tablet on her lap. "Fanchon to *Orion* mission support," she said quietly into her headset. "We need your assistance locating a team member, and we hear Emmett has experience in doing this..."

The professor and the mission team clustered around Fanchon. Restless, Cruz began to walk the length of the thicket, using his MC camera to search for Bryndis.

As Cruz paced, something caught his attention. It was one of the smaller gorillas. She was moving parallel to his position. The group of gorillas had been here for almost an hour. They were probably getting ready to move on. Another gorilla was following the first. Four of the younger gorillas in the group had formed a semicircle. They were looking down, furrowing their heavy brows and twitching wrinkled noses. The way they were tilting their heads, it was almost like they had found something...

Bryndis!

Cruz had to stop himself from bolting across the meadow. He was about 50 feet from the team, near where the group had stowed their equipment. It was too far to yell without upsetting the gorillas. Cruz fumbled to put his earpiece in.

"...and Taryn says we've been getting intermittent readings from her OS band since you guys left the ship," he heard Emmett say. "Tracking her could be difficult if the band is broken, but I'll do my best."

"Emmett! Everybody!" Cruz cut into the conversation. "I've spotted Bryndis. At least, I think I have. She's on the ground near the group of gorillas."

Emmett didn't respond. Cruz glanced up. No one from Fanchon's group spoke or turned.

"When was your last full bio reading?" Fanchon was asking.

"Uh...hold on," said Emmett. "We're checking."

Hadn't anyone heard him?

"Hello? Emmett? Fanchon?" Cruz's headset must be malfunctioning. He could run back to his team, but it would waste valuable time. If Bryndis was sick, then she was also exposing the gorillas to her germs. For her health, as well as that of the animals, he needed to get her out of there. Now!

Cruz's gaze fell to the spare hoods and gloves resting on top of Fanchon's pack.

Did he dare...?

Cruz lunged for the gear. He could barely breathe, let alone think. He tried to remember everything the team had done and the order in which they had done it. His hands were shaking so much, he could barely take off his comm and GPS pins. Cruz dropped them in his pocket. He pulled on the gloves and hood. Trying to slow his breathing and his thoughts, Cruz tapped his shadow badge twice. As the morphing process began, he felt a hand on his shoulder.

"What are you doing?" Shristine gasped, everything but her head and hands still cloaked. The floating head of Felipe was beside her.

"Saving Bryndis," said Cruz. "The gorillas found her. I know where she is."

"Professor Ishikawa, Cruz says he thinks he knows where Bryndis is,"

Felipe whispered into his headset. "Permission to go get her?"

"What did...? Fanchon is...Hold on a minute," said their instructor. At least, that's as much as Cruz heard. He pulled out his earpiece. "My headset is cutting out. There's no time to explain except to say it's a health emergency. If you're going with me, we have to go."

"I'm in," said Shristine.

"Me too," said Felipe.

They put on their hoods and gloves.

"We've trained for this, so we know what to do," Shristine said to Cruz. "Hold hands. That way, we can stay together while we're cloaked."

Cruz felt her fingers slide into his palm. He heard Felipe move in behind her.

"You lead us, Cruz, since you know where we're going," said Shristine. "Squeeze my hand when you are ready to stop. I will pass the message along to Felipe by squeezing his hand. If you have to speak, keep it low. Everybody clear?"

"Check," said Felipe.

"Check," squeaked Cruz.

Off they went, half walking, half jogging across the meadow. When Cruz was within a few yards of the gorillas, he squeezed Shristine's hand once. She returned the squeeze. Cruz inched his way toward the animals. They were seated in a semicircle, fascinated by a spot on the ground between them. They didn't seem angry or scared. Merely curious. As Cruz approached, their heads turned slightly and probing brown eyes seemed to look directly at him. But that was impossible. Wasn't it?

Cruz knelt near where it looked like the grass had been flattened. Still holding Shristine's fingers in his right hand, he began to feel along the ground with his left. Inch by inch, he began patting the wet grass.

Patting...patting...patting...

His thumb smacked something. He felt it with his palm. It was rubber and notched—the sole of Bryndis's boot!

Cruz pulled Shristine's hand so she could feel the shoe, too. By the way

Bryndis's legs were positioned, he could tell she was lying on her right side. "I'm going to her left," he whispered to Shristine. "Take Felipe to her right. We'll try and get her up."

Shristine squeezed his hand once to confirm, then let go.

Cruz crawled along the back of Bryndis, touching her leg, her arm, her shoulder, and her neck. He lowered his head close to where he thought her ear should be. "Bryndis?"

She let out a soft moan.

"Can you walk?"

She coughed. "I'll...try."

Carefully lifting a limp arm, he placed it around his neck. By the impressions on the grass across from him, Cruz could tell that Shristine and Felipe had made it to her other side. Together, the three of them got Bryndis up. She clung to Cruz and tried to walk, but she had no strength. She was like a limp doll. Her feet were dragging. Cruz, Felipe, and Shristine had to bear most of her weight. They staggered slowly back the way they'd come. By the time they laid Bryndis on the ground behind the brush, Cruz was panting. He yanked off his hood first, then gently peeled back the one on Bryndis.

Her face was an ashy white. The corners of her lips were blue. Her breathing was shallow and raspy. She was shivering. What could be wrong? And how in the world could they possibly help her out here in the middle of a cloud forest?

Pained blue eyes searched his. "I sprayed them..." wheezed Bryndis. "My...my gorillas...tell Professor...mission complete."

"I will." Cruz choked back a swell of emotions. "Take it easy. You were great. You're safe now, and everything's going to be okay. Bryndis? *Bryndis?*"

She was lifeless in his arms.

11

CRUZ WAS THE LAST one

off the helicopter.

The second his feet hit the tip of the giant letter *A* on *Orion*'s helipad, Cruz made a dash for the observation roost. The hike out of the forest, the night at the research center, the drive to Kisoro, the flight on *Condor*—they came home exactly the same way they had gone, yet it seemed like it had taken twice as long. The worst part was that the only news they'd heard about Bryndis was that the doctors in Kampala were doing everything they could, which was no news at all. Cruz was hoping that, by now, Taryn or Aunt Marisol had heard something from Fanchon.

The tech lab chief had flown with Bryndis to the hospital. Cruz would never forget the look on Fanchon's face as the medevac helicopter had lifted off from the meadow. Through the window, their eyes had connected, and Cruz had seen something he couldn't recall ever seeing in Fanchon Quills: fear. The genius scientist who wasn't the least bit afraid of venomous creatures, dangerous chemicals, or pulsing blobs of . . . whatever was in her sensotivia gel . . . was scared now.

Cruz hurried into the small oval nest of a room on *Orion*'s top deck. He expected to see his teammates or, at the very least, Aunt Marisol. They weren't there. The only person who *was* there was Dr. Eikenboom. He was wearing a hazmat suit with a hood. As Cruz entered, he saw Professor Ishikawa, Shristine, Felipe, and Ali putting on masks and gloves.

Dr. Eikenboom handed a set to Cruz. "You're officially in quarantine. You are all to report to sick bay immediately."

"All of us?" asked Cruz. He pointed to Captain Roxas, who was wheeling in the cart with duffel bags and backpacks. "What about—"

"Him, too, as well as the flight crew of the *Condor*."

Shristine tilted her head. "Quarantine—what does that mean?"

"It means we can't go back to our cabins," said Felipe.

Ali groaned. "Not even to shower?"

"You'll be in quarantine until we pinpoint what caused Bryndis to collapse," explained Dr. Eikenboom, pressing the button for the elevator.

"How is she?" asked Cruz.

"Holding her own," said the ship's doctor solemnly.

What did that mean? Cruz was too afraid to ask. He felt his chest tighten. It had been more than 24 hours. They should have figured out what was wrong with her by now!

"Leave your packs, duffels, and everything here," instructed Dr. Eikenboom when Cruz reached for his bag. "We'll take care of it. My team is waiting for you in sick bay."

Wriggling his fingers into the second glove, Cruz got into the elevator. Professor Ishikawa stepped in and stood next to him. Cruz kept his eyes down. He knew his teacher was upset with him. Not that he had said as much. Truth was, Professor Ishikawa had hardly spoken to Cruz on the journey home, which only confirmed he *was* mad. Normally, Cruz would have waited for the go-ahead from the professor to put a rescue plan into motion, but in this case, there wasn't time. Yet, Cruz was the only one who knew that.

The elevator door opened. Professor Ishikawa got off ahead of Cruz without so much as a glance his way.

Pendrina Antonov, Dr. Eikenboom's physician's assistant, greeted them in the reception area. She also wore a hazmat jumpsuit. "Hello, everyone, good to see you," said Pendrina. Blue eyes peered out the clear, rectangular windshield of her hood. "Don't mind the suit. It's precautionary only. Please follow me. You'll each need to shower," she instructed as they headed past the exam rooms. "We only have the one shower, so you'll have to take turns. We'll need all your clothes and uniforms so they can be thoroughly cleaned."

One by one, they showered and changed into the fresh clothes Pendrina had waiting. For the explorers: EA tees, sweatpants, and gray fuzzy slipper socks. Before handing over his uniform, Cruz slipped his mom's journal and the octopod out of his jacket and into the pockets of his sweats. He started to remove his comm pin, too, but Pendrina caught him. She shook her smooth, rubbery head. "Sorry." She held out a palm. "We need to sanitize all pins and badges, too. You'll get them back, along with your uniform, backpack, and duffel bag, tomorrow."

Sighing, Cruz dropped his comm pin into her hand, then followed her into an exam room.

"Your OS band indicates your vitals are normal, which is good," said the physician's assistant, "but we want to double-check." She took his temperature on his forehead, peered into his ears and mouth, and listened to his heart and lungs. "Are you having any of the following: dizziness, weakness, chills, fever, difficulty breathing, or nausea?"

Cruz put a hand to his growling stomach. "Does hunger count?"

Pendrina grinned. "Let's get you settled in first, then we'll have Chef Kristos send up something. We're almost done. I want to look at your OS data for the past few days." Her eyebrows slowly came together as she reviewed the info, but after a few minutes Pendrina seemed satisfied that Cruz was healthy. She turned him over to another nurse named Richelle.

"Come with me, please," said Richelle,

who was also wearing a protective suit. She led him out of the exam room and past the nurses' station to a heavy glass door at the end of the hall. The sign outside read Q BAY 1–2.

"Home sweet home." Richelle unlocked the door using a keypad and waved him in.

A few feet inside the room were two more glass doors, one leading to the left half of the room and the other to the right. A thick transparent partition separated the two sides. The nurse directed Cruz to the right side, Q1. He took a quick look around—not that there was much more to see than a twin bed and an airplane-size bathroom. At the head of his bed was a nook in the wall, and above it, a round reading light. There were no portholes. Three walls and the ceiling were covered in stainless steel. It was like being in a giant sink. There was even a drain on the floor between the beds.

"We'll be monitoring your OS band," said Richelle. "It feeds into the computer at the nurses' station. One of us will check in on you regularly, but if you start to feel unwell or need anything, don't hesitate to press the red button by the bed, okay?"

"Okay."

"The blue button allows you to talk to your mate in Q2. There's also a tablet in the nook in the wall..."

A tablet? Cruz scrambled for it.

"You can check out an e-book from the library, play games, listen to music, do your homework, or whatever you want..."

Who should he call? Emmett? Lani? It was probably a good idea to touch base with Aunt Marisol and his dad first. Cruz's eyes darted over the screen, searching for the video call icon.

"About the only thing you can't do is contact anyone," said Richelle.

His head popped up. "I can't?"

"We want our patients to rest."

"But I have to get ahold of—"

"Your aunt, your family, your roommate, and your adviser have all been notified of the situation. Relax, Cruz. We'll release you as soon as we know it's safe to do so." Richelle stepped out of the room, and the door slid shut.

"Release." The word made him feel like a prisoner. The locking door did not help. Lying on his back, Cruz lifted his wrist to inspect his OS band. He really needed to get Emmett to show him how to hack into this thing. Turning his head, he looked through the glass partition. The other bay was identical to his own. There was a curtain on each side that you could pull for privacy. Cruz left his side open. He wondered who his roommate would be: Ali, Felipe, or—gulp—Professor Ishikawa.

Cruz reached for the tablet, logged on to his account, and started reading his assignment on food chains for biology. He was going to have to be nothing less than perfect to get back in Professor Ishikawa's good graces. He read about decomposers, organisms that break down dead organic material, like earthworms, slugs, crabs, and vultures. It was interesting stuff, but he couldn't seem to focus. Cruz would read a page, then have to read it again. He set the tablet aside.

The outer door to the two quarantine bays was opening.

It was Richelle again. She had Ali with her. "Home sweet home," she said, pointing to the left bay and giving him the same speech she had given Cruz. When Richelle left, Ali flopped onto the bed on his back.

Cruz hit the blue comm button. "Hey, Q2. Looks like we're roommates, at least for a while, huh?"

"Yeah." Ali threw an arm over his face.

"You okay?"

"Not really."

Cruz sat up. "Should I call—"

"I'm not sick."

He must be worried. "Are you scared we might get sick?" pressed Cruz.

Ali didn't answer. Guess he was. Guess he didn't want to talk about it. Cruz plumped up his pillow. He smoothed out his blanket. He wound a loose string on the toe of his sock around his index finger. Yep, totally bored.

"Stupid me." Ali slid his arm aside. "I actually thought I was ahead. For once."

Cruz unwound the thread. "What do you mean?"

"You haven't noticed? Nah, why would you?"

Cruz didn't know what Ali was talking about.

"Everyone else figures things out before I do," said Ali, staring at the metal ceiling. "I don't think of a good question to ask in class until *after* the bell rings ... or how to win a game until *after* I lose. But when I got on the mission team to help the gorillas, I finally felt like I wasn't playing catch-up. For once, I was ahead, you know?"

"Yeah, I guess."

"And then you pushed me back again."

"Me?" Cruz sat taller. "How did I—"

Ali went up on his elbows. "I should have been the one to help save Bryndis. I was a member of the mission team. Not you."

"I know, Ali, but everything happened so fast—"

"If Dr. Vanderwick hadn't been sick, you wouldn't have even gotten to come along. You were in the right place at the right time, that's all."

He couldn't deny it. That much was true.

"Wasn't that good enough for you, to be part of the team?" Ali's voice was getting louder. Angrier. "Did you have to steal my spot, too?"

In a flash, Cruz was at the clear wall that separated them. "That wasn't what ... I never thought ... I didn't mean to replace you on the team."

"But you did."

"I'm sorry, Ali ... All that mattered was getting to Bryndis ... She needed me—us."

"More like you needed her."

Cruz felt his temper bubbling. "What's that supposed to mean?"

"It means you saw your chance and grabbed it—stole it, is more like it."

"I would have included you if you'd come with Shristine and Felipe. We could have all gone together—"

"But we didn't. You know what you are, Cruz? You're a hero hog."

"A *what*?"

"You know, someone who has to show off and save the day, no matter what, even if it means hurting someone else. Like me."

"That's not true. I never meant to—"

"It's done. It's over. And you can't fix it, so forget it. Q2 comm, off." Ali whirled to face the wall. He punched his pillow into submission. The lamp in Q2 went dark.

Cruz stood there, staring at Ali's back. Did Ali really think that Cruz would deliberately exclude him? Guess so. Cruz didn't know what to do to fix things. He felt awful.

Cruz shuffled into the bathroom to brush his teeth, then got into bed. The last thing he did was pull off his slipper socks and drop them on the floor. "Light, out."

In the darkness, Cruz stared at the lump in the opposite bed. How could he make Ali understand that he hadn't meant to replace him on the team? In all the excitement, it had just…

Happened.

Professor Ishikawa was upset with him. Ali was upset with him. When the rest of the explorers heard Ali's version of the story, they'd probably be mad, too.

Flipping over to face the stainless-steel wall, Cruz curled up into a ball. When Richelle came with a dinner tray, he pretended to be asleep. He wasn't hungry anymore anyway.

CRUZ FELT THE FLICKER OF LIGHT against his closed eyes and, for a moment, thought he had fallen asleep with his head against the car window. He couldn't remember where his dad and he were going. Was it to Nawiliwili for some gourmet ice cream? His dad always got pog sorbet, a combination of passion fruit, orange, and guava. Cruz always chose macadamia nut. In the car on the way there, Cruz would talk about trying something new like ginger cream or ube, which was made from yams and was bright purple, but in the end, he always got macadamia nut. It was the safe choice. Cruz's eyelids fluttered, then opened.

There was no car, no sunlight being dappled by trees, no ice cream.

He was still in the sink room, and it was dark but for the beam of flashlight playing over his face. Cruz could see at least two heads on the other side of the glass door; however, the dim hallway light cast them in shadows. He couldn't be totally sure who was there, but he had a pretty good idea.

Cruz shaded his eyes with one hand and tossed off his covers with the other. As the balls of his feet hit the cold floor, it sent a tremor up his spine. As Cruz had suspected, it was Emmett and Sailor. His OS band read 12:19 a.m. How had they managed to get past the nurses' station? Since Lani wasn't with them, he had a feeling she was in charge of their diversionary strategy.

Emmett pointed to the speaker button next to the door, which would have allowed them to communicate, shook his head, and motioned behind him. Cruz understood. They had to keep silent to avoid alerting the duty nurse, who sat behind her computer not far from the outside door.

Sailor held up her tablet. Bold neon green letters on a black screen read: *Are you okay?*

Cruz gave them a thumbs-up before scurrying to get his tablet to ask a question of his own: *Is Bryndis all right?*

They shrugged.

Emmett typed a message on his tablet: *We'll tell you if we hear anything.*

"Thanks," mouthed Cruz.

Sailor was holding up her screen again: *By the way, no fair decoding the clue and keeping it a secret!*

Cruz stifled a laugh. He *knew* that would drive her nuts.

Sailor was typing again. She gave him a smirk, as she stuck her screen up against the glass: *Namibia.*

His jaw fell. She knew!

You figured it out, too? typed Cruz.

Sailor gave a confident nod, even as Emmett vigorously shook his head.

A realization striking him, Cruz typed a new phrase: *Aunt Marisol?*

Emmett's oval glasses were turning bright pink. Cruz was right! His aunt *had* told them.

Another message from Emmett's tablet: *Where in Namibia?*

It was Cruz's turn to shrug.

Emmett typed another note: *We'll figure it out.*

Sailor lifted her tablet again. *Lani says hi. She's distracting the nurse from a remote location.*

Cruz shook his head to ask in the only way he could: How was she doing that? He soon had his answer. *She hacked into the sick bay computer. Now the nurse is trying to figure out why Chef Kristos's recipe for double-fudge brownies keeps popping up on her screen.*

Cruz snickered.

Emmett was glancing down at his tablet, gray bubbles swirling through his emoto-frames. He turned to Sailor, and Cruz was able to read his lips. "We have to go!"

Sailor planted her palm flat against the glass. She didn't need to mouth any words or type on her tablet. Her look said it all. She was glad to see him. Cruz put his hand over hers. He hoped his own expression said he was glad they'd come. She stepped back. Emmett made a fist and put his knuckles against the clear pane. Cruz did the same, tapping his knuckles to Emmett's.

His friends hurried out, slipping into a side passage before reaching the nurses' station. Cruz had no idea where it went, but he had no doubt Emmett did. His roommate loved schematics. One day, Cruz would ask Emmett what he knew about the mystery door on B deck and the woman Mell had observed.

Cruz made it over to his bed with only three leaps on the chilled floor.

Slipping beneath the covers, he couldn't stop grinning. Chef Kristos's recipe for brownies! Lani was too funny. And risking the wrath of Taryn and the nurses to sneak in and check on him? It was risky. It was crazy. It was...

Wonderful.

12

WHEN CRUZ AWOKE,

the bed across from him was empty.

Ali's bathroom door was open, and the light was off. Cruz pressed his call button three times. He tugged on his slipper socks, not caring they were inside out, and hurried to glue himself to the glass door. A figure was approaching, a blond man wearing a gray short-sleeved V-neck shirt and matching pants. No mask. No gloves. No hazmat suit. Once he was through the first door, Cruz got a look at his badge: B. Gunnar, R.N. The nurse pressed the speaker outside of Cruz's room, and a deep voice said, "Good morning. What can I get you for breakfast?"

"Where's Ali?" cried Cruz. "What's going on? Is he sick?"

"Ali is fine," drawled Gunnar. "He woke up early, had breakfast, and we sent him on his way. Doc says you can go, too, once you've had something to eat."

"So then ..." Cruz put a hand to his chest. "I'm all right?"

"Right as rain." As if to prove it, Gunnar tapped the keypad, and the door separating them slid open.

It was true. Cruz really was free!

"And Bryndis?" Cruz held his breath.

"Nothing to report, I'm afraid," answered Gunnar. "But don't read too much into that. We won't hear any details unless her family gives Dr. Hightower permission to share them."

Cruz gave a nod. He caught a glimpse of the time on his OS band. It was 8:29. "Uh-oh. I'm missing class."

"No, you're not," said Gunnar. "With Professor Ishikawa and the five of you in here and Professor Benedict and four other explorers down with colds, Taryn thought it was best to postpone classes for today. Now, let's try this again. What would you like for breakfast?"

Cruz ordered scrambled eggs and toast but couldn't seem to manage more than a few bites of either. He was washing down breakfast with some ice-cold milk when, through the hazy bottom of his glass, a dark-haired figure in pink appeared.

His glass hit the tray with a crash. "Aunt Marisol!"

Cruz shoved the rolling tray table away. Before he could even get off the bed, she was next to him, her arms around him. His aunt held him tight and far longer than usual. She released him. "You're all right?"

"Yep. Perfect."

"Professor Ishikawa told me what happened at Bwindi. You actually ran into the meadow under the cover of your shadow badge to bring out Bryndis?"

"With Shristine and Felipe," he added.

His aunt chuckled. "What are you, some kind of superhero?"

"I'm not a hero, Aunt Marisol. The truth is ... what happened with Bryndis ... I could have prevented it."

She pulled back. "I don't understand."

"I knew Bryndis wasn't feeling good. She tried to pretend everything was okay, but I could see it wasn't ..." He wrung his hands. "She was so excited to see the gorillas, and I ... I thought if something was really wrong, her OS band would alert Taryn."

"It should have," said his aunt. "Unfortunately, we were having trouble getting *any* readings from your bands. I don't know if it was the distance, elevation, or a technical glitch, but it also prevented us from being able to locate Bryndis using her band when she went missing."

His aunt touched his arm. "Don't be so hard on yourself. Everyone gets aches and pains. You didn't know it was something more serious."

Maybe not, but knowing that didn't make Cruz feel better.

Aunt Marisol glanced around at his stainless-steel cell. "The nurse said you could leave once you'd had some breakfast. Are you sure you're done?"

"Uh-huh."

She looked at his nearly full plate. "Something else on your mind?"

"It's just...I dread facing everybody. Professor Ishikawa is mad and—"

"He isn't mad." Lifting her hand, she put a tiny space between her thumb and index finger. "Okay, maybe a teeny bit, but it's only because it's his job on the mission to look out for *everyone's* safety. He didn't want you taking unnecessary risks. But he also knows you were worried and couldn't help acting impulsively. And I'm sure he remembers what it's like to be young and..." She bit her lower lip, the way you do when you are trying to keep from grinning.

"What?"

She let the smile win. "In love."

"Aunt Marisol!"

"I've seen how you look at Bryndis." She wiggled her eyebrows. "And how she looks back."

"Oh, *maaaaaan.*" Embarrassed, Cruz slapped a hand over his eyes and fell backward onto the mattress.

She got to her feet. "We've got work to do. But not here." She pointed down. "My office."

She meant his mom's clue.

Cruz was ready to leave sick bay now!

"I have no idea where in Namibia I'm supposed to go," confessed Cruz the second his aunt shut her office door. "I was hoping you could help. Do you know if Mom had a friend in Namibia? Maybe she did some research there?"

Aunt Marisol sank into her desk chair. "Nothing comes to mind, but I can check into it."

Cruz wondered if that meant she was going to pay a visit to Jericho and the rest of the Synthesis scientists in the belly of the ship. Crossing the small office, Cruz looked out the porthole. He'd missed having a view—not that he could see much more than the silhouette of flat dunes and rocky outcrops in the distance. Still, the ocean was a hundred times better than metal walls. "Where are we?" he asked.

"Off the coast of Somalia," answered his aunt. "We've rounded the Horn of Africa. We'll reach the port of Mombasa in a couple of days."

Once the explorers deployed the SHOT-bots in the Serengeti, they'd likely be leaving Africa, unless they had a reason to stay. Cruz needed to pinpoint a destination in Namibia. And fast. He was already planning when he could watch his mom's clue again with his friends.

His aunt's tablet was chiming.

"Hello, Marisol."

Cruz recognized the voice.

"Dr. Hightower!" Aunt Marisol straightened. So did Cruz. "This is a pleasant surprise."

"I wish it were," said the schoolmaster.

"Is there a problem?"

"A rather serious one, I'm afraid. Has Cruz received any threats or communication from Nebula recently?"

"Nebula?" Aunt Marisol's head went up, and mocha eyes burned into his.

Cruz shook his head vigorously.

Her eyes became slits. Translation: *You'd better be telling me the truth.*

Cruz made an X over his heart.

His aunt glanced down. "No, Dr. Hightower. Nothing. Not since the kidnapping."

"I see." Dr. Hightower sounded disappointed. "It dawned on me that this was the kind of thing they might be behind. I was hoping there was some explanation for it, but ..."

"What's going on, Regina?"

"It involves what happened to Bryndis."

Cruz jumped.

"Bryndis?" Aunt Marisol frowned. "We're all quite worried about her, naturally, but I don't understand. I thought she was ill. What do you mean by 'happened to' her? What does Nebula—"

"I need your word that you will keep this strictly between us." Dr. Hightower lowered her voice. "I don't want to create a panic among the explorers or their families."

Aunt Marisol looked over her tablet at Cruz. He held up his hand, swearing he would keep whatever he heard a secret.

"Absolutely," said his aunt. "It goes no further than this cabin."

"On the mission in Uganda, Bryndis was exposed to a deadly toxin," said Dr. Hightower. "The poison was absorbed through her skin."

Both Cruz and his aunt gasped.

"She's been given the only antidote available, but it's effective less than half the time," continued Dr. Hightower. "We've got a team of our top Society scientists working round the clock to try to find an alternative ..."

"How did this happen?" asked Aunt Marisol.

"That's what we're trying to figure out. At first, we thought a container from Fanchon's gear may have leaked into Bryndis's luggage on the helicopter or airplane. But Fanchon assured me she was not transporting any hazardous materials, and a thorough inspection of her cases, her field lab, and even the tech lab on *Orion* turned up nothing. I'm convinced she was not the source. On the other hand, my team says it's unlikely Bryndis would have come in contact with such a powerful poison by accident," said Dr. Hightower. "To me, it has all the markings of

Nebula, but perhaps I've watched one too many murder mysteries..."

Cruz felt a light tap on the back of his neck. It was his aunt's floating heart clocks. The trio of hearts could be set adrift to aimlessly float around the room (a base unit on her desk kept them from leaving the office). However, they were linked horizontally with tiny chains so that wherever they went, they had to travel together. The first clock told the current time on *Orion*, the second clock had the time in Hawaii, and the third clock gave the time in Washington, D.C. Cruz reached out for the hearts, turning them so he could see their faces. The first clock read 10:18 a.m.; the second, 9:18 p.m.; the third, 3:18 a.m.

It was the middle of the night back at the Academy. No wonder Dr. Hightower sounded so tired. She probably hadn't slept much since hearing about Bryndis. If there was one thing Cruz had discovered about the president of the Academy, it was that she deeply cared and felt responsible for each and every one of her explorers.

Cruz set his aunt's heart clocks free.

"It's quite a puzzle," Dr. Hightower was saying. "My security team here and those on board *Orion* will be continuing the investigation. I'll alert them that you've been briefed on the situation. They may be in touch."

"Of course," said Aunt Marisol. "And please tell Bryndis and her family that everyone on *Orion* is thinking about her and pulling for her." Her eyes met Cruz's. "We all love her and miss her."

Cruz's eyes were welling up. He did his best to blink away the tears.

"Thank you, I will," said Dr. Hightower.

Cruz couldn't believe it. Bryndis hadn't done anything differently from the rest of the explorers, had she?

"...I'm on my way to the hospital to offer my support to Bryndis and her family," said the school president. "As soon as *Condor* lands, which should be any minute, I'll be off..."

Condor. What was it Dr. Hightower had said earlier about the plane? Something about thinking Fanchon's case had leaked onto Bryndis's bag during the flight...

A thousand tiny hairs on the back of Cruz's neck suddenly stood at attention.

No! NO!

Cruz lunged forward. "Ask her where they found it," he hissed to his aunt.

She squinted. "Wh-what?"

"*Where* did they find the poison?"

"Uh... Dr. Hightower, before you go," said Aunt Marisol, "we—I—was curious, do you know how Bryndis was exposed to the toxin?"

"Didn't I mention that? I'm sorry... They traced it to her duffel bag... It was on some of her clothes and socks."

Cruz felt every ounce of strength drain from his body. He slumped against the tiny red sofa, and if it hadn't been there, would have probably oozed to the floor. Somehow, Cruz managed to sit down. He grabbed the little white pillow with the cross-stitched crown from the corner of the sofa and clung to it like a life preserver.

"...we checked all the rest of the bags and backpacks, and they were clean," continued the Academy president. "So how it got there and only there, we don't know."

"Let's hope you get some answers soon," said his aunt. "Keep me posted, and safe travels."

The second the call ended, Aunt Marisol came flying around the desk. "You're as pale as white limestone. What's going on? Tell me the truth, Cruz. Has Nebula contacted you?"

"No," he croaked. "I wasn't lying about that."

"So what's going on?"

"I didn't think it was any big deal ... if I had I would never ... There was no threat ... no message ... nothing ... It's my fault ... It's because of me ..."

"Cruz?" Aunt Marisol grabbed his upper arm, as if to shake one clear thought from him.

He took a deep breath. "The zipper was broken on Bryndis's duffel bag. So for the mission, I loaned her mine."

"That means ... you're saying ..." Her voice fizzled out like a dud firework.

Cruz said what his aunt could not. "The poison was meant for me."

➤PRESCOTT'S PHONE *was*

rumbling its way across the gray weathered-wood table. He had wedged himself into a corner seat in what had to be the tiniest coffee shop in all of London to relax with tea and a blueberry scone.

Let Zebra wait.

Sinking an antique spoon into the piping hot oolong tea with milk and honey, Prescott slowly stirred the liquid. The silver spoon made a delicate tink-tink sound against the porcelain. He inhaled the rich, fruity steam. A few feet from his redbrick corner was a rain-spattered bay window. Holiday shoppers scuttled past in the light shower, juggling their bags and umbrellas, or brollies, as the British call them. It must be nice to have someone to buy things for. Lifting the blue-and-white-floral china cup to his lips, Prescott felt the hot, rich tea slide over his tongue. He was starting to think about change. Not seriously. Not yet. But now and then, in the quiet moments, a thought would slip into his head, a thought that there might be something better than this.

His phone was dancing again. Could he not have a moment's peace? Prescott jabbed at the screen.

Assignment FAILED.
Right poison. Wrong explorer.
Complication has arisen.
Have alerted Lion.
Explanation to come.
Regretfully, Z

Irritated, Prescott answered with a quick affirmative, then turned his phone off. This assignment was starting to leave a sour taste in his mouth that not even tea could take away. Worse, it was his fault. If he had done his job right the first time . . . or the second time . . . or the third . . .

"Good afternoon."

Surprised, Prescott's knuckles hit the gold handle of his cup, sending tea sloshing over the rim. His fingers burning, Prescott did not flinch. He gazed up at the man standing in front of his table: Malcolm Rook, the former Academy head librarian and former Nebula spy. Code name: Meerkat. Rook had dyed his red hair a muddy brown. He'd also shaved off his beard and lost a few pounds. But those cocky green eyes? They were still the same.

"I have a proposition for you." Rook dug into the pocket of a wrinkled, drab green jacket. He tossed a holo-business card onto the table. "If you're interested, watch it."

"Bold of you," Prescott said drily. "Considering who you are. And who I am."

Rook did not change expression, but a little muscle in his jaw began to twitch. Prescott had hit a nerve. Good. He wanted Rook to be scared. He wanted him to crawl back into the hole he'd crawled out of. If he didn't and Brume discovered it, Prescott would have to make sure Rook never did it again.

Prescott did not move.

Rook bent. "Ask yourself, if Lion is going to such lengths to destroy it, what must it be worth to him? Or to someone else?"

Turning on his heel, Rook was out the door of the tearoom in three strides. Once outside, he crossed Frith Street, slid between two parked cars, and disappeared around the first corner.

Meerkat was still the same. Sneaky. Greedy. And completely untrustworthy. However, he did have a point.

Prescott ate every crumb of his blueberry scone and swallowed every last drop of tea. Sliding out from behind his corner seat, he stood and put on his coat. It was raining harder. He had no brolly. Prescott reached for the holo-card. His gut told him to rip it in half.

His gut was telling him a lot of things these days he was ignoring.

14

HEARING A SOFT TAP,

Cruz went to open the door of his cabin. "Hi."

"Hi," said Lani and Sailor, their expressions as somber as his own.

Cruz stepped back to let the girls into cabin 202. Sailor gave him a quick hug.

Lani bumped his shoulder gently with hers. "Any news about Bryndis?"

Cruz shook his head. It was hard to keep what he knew from his friends, but he *had* promised.

Sailor sank into her favorite chair. "How about the gorillas?"

"Professor Ishikawa said he'll let us know when he has an update and to stop bothering him about it," sighed Emmett.

Cruz sat cross-legged on the floor, leaving the other chair for Lani. Instead of taking it, she plopped down next to him. Emmett, who was about to scoot his desk chair into the circle, saw the open navy chair and took it.

Going up on his knees, Cruz laid his mom's journal on the round table. "All right, we're looking for something that gives us a location in Namibia, so look carefully. Shout if you see *anything* that might help us." He pressed his thumb to the corner of the page to activate the holo-journal. Seconds later, flaps appeared and the paper transformed into a multi-pointed sphere. Once the morphing and identification sequences were complete, they all leaned in to focus.

"You'll know where to go once you solve this cryptogram," said Cruz's mom, pointing to the cluster of boxes that had appeared in front of her. "By now you've seen it thousands of times. It's as familiar as a rainbow. One word of advice: Use all your senses. Good luck, Cruzer."

As before, the boxes in color began to move forward and back in the same order they had before: a red 25, a green 8, a purple 11, a yellow 26 ...

Cruz didn't get it. He'd decoded the boxes that made up the colors of the light spectrum, yet they were still missing a specific destination. Should they be paying attention to the other boxes? The ones that were clear? And if so, which ones? None of them were moving.

"I don't see anything different from last time," moaned Sailor.

"That's it!" Lani gasped. "Don't look. Listen!"

Everyone froze.

Chirp, chirp. Chirp, chirp.

The tweeting bird! Cruz hadn't given much thought to it, figuring his mom had probably made the recording near a window or something. Now he was beginning to understand. That's what his mother had meant when she'd said to use all his senses. The chirps were part of the clue!

Emmett scrambled to get to his bank of computers. "Cruz, send me the video you took of the clue. I'll plug the audio of the bird's chirping into the library's bird-identification software."

"Maybe it leads to another wildlife sanctuary," said Sailor, "like Freyja's Cloak."

"Or a park like Bwindi," said Lani.

"I hope it leads somewhere." Cruz hit the send button. "And soon."

"It shouldn't take long to get a match," said Emmett. "This software can scan thousands of birds in a few minutes."

Someone was knocking on the door. Cruz went to open it.

"Special delivery." Taryn held Cruz's shoes in one hand and his uniform, pressed and neatly folded, in the other. Hubbard was with her, carrying his green ball.

Cruz reached to give the pup a quick scratch behind the ears before taking his things. "Thanks." Perched on his clothes was a three-by-five-inch white box.

"Your pins," explained Taryn. "All bright and shiny. Your backpack is still being cleaned, and your duffel ... well, I'm not sure what happened to that. Laundry can't seem to locate it."

Cruz fidgeted. He bet his duffel was probably still with Dr. Hightower's security team.

"I don't know how you can lose something that big," said his adviser. "If it doesn't turn up soon, I'll order you a new one."

"It doesn't matter," said Cruz, more harshly than he'd meant to. He had more important things on his mind. "How is Bryndis?"

She shook her pixie cut, but her face said she knew something.

"Come on, Taryn." Emmett was at Cruz's shoulder, his shape-shifting frames sapphire blue teardrops of determination.

Turning, Cruz saw that Sailor had come to stand behind Emmett, and Lani was stretching to peer out from behind Sailor.

"You must have heard by now," pressed Sailor.

"At least, tell us what's wrong," said Lani.

Taryn bit her lip. "I really can't ..."

"Pleeeease," begged Sailor, her voice breaking. Bryndis was her roommate, teammate, and best friend.

Glancing from one concerned face to the next, Taryn let out that sigh parents give when they are out of excuses. She shooed them back into the room, stepped inside with Hubbard, and shut the door. "This stays between us for now. She had some sort of allergic reaction. She's in serious condition. That's all I know. Honest."

Taryn sounded sincere, but she could be lying as a favor to Dr. Hightower. Was she lying about not knowing what happened to his duffel, too?

"I know you want to protect us, but we can take it, even if it's bad news," said Emmett, the blues in his glasses fading to a more contented green.

"It's worse when we don't know," interjected Sailor with a sniffle.

Taryn gave a sympathetic nod. "Once I have more information and permission from her parents, I'll make an announcement to all the explorers."

They thanked her, and Taryn and Hubbard left.

Emmett was bounding across the room. The screen on one of his computers was flashing. "It's done. The software has finished its analysis."

"And?" Cruz clasped his hands. "What kind of bird is it?"

"It isn't." Emmett frowned. "It isn't a bird."

"That's crazy," said Sailor. "It's chirping. It *has* to be a bird."

"Not according to this."

Sailor marched to him to examine the report, then declared, "He's right."

"Maybe it's a bird that's extinct," said Lani. "Like the Spix's macaw or the passenger pigeon."

"If it lived within the last two hundred years, it's in the database," said Emmett. "I'm telling you, it's not a bird."

Sailor yanked on her ponytail. "Then what is it?"

"Beats me."

It was getting late. The girls said their good nights and headed back to their cabins.

While Emmett got into his pajamas, Cruz put his uniform back in the closet. He lifted the lid from the box Taryn had given him. Inside, his GPS pin, comm pin, shadow badge, and the remote for Mell rested in a nest of cotton. Closing the lid, he set the box on his nightstand so he wouldn't forget to put the pins back on his uniform in the morning. With his foot, he slid his shoes under his bed. One of them hit something. He knew what it was. Cruz bent, reached an arm under the bed, and brought out the aqua box that held his mother's things. As he often did, Cruz took inventory of its contents: a bag of almonds, a gold jewelry box key, a silver Aztec crown charm, the photo of himself with the swirl cipher on the back, a box of bandages, a pad of cat-shaped sticky notes, two washers (one ridged, one smooth), three pencils, four pens, a clip, a stapler, an eraser, and a yellow lined pad. There was also

Cruz's addition: the clay deer from the lost stone city in Turkey. Yep, it was all there.

It seemed weird that this was all that had survived from the lab fire. What about computer files, video logs, holo-notebooks, or even regular notebooks? There had to be more. After all, his mother was a founding member of the Synthesis. She must have worked on dozens of projects over the years before her research into venoms led to developing her cell-regeneration serum. It was probably all top secret stuff, though—

Cruz froze.

Venoms were poisons secreted by animals. Science had created numerous antidotes to counteract these poisons, like the one Dr. Hightower had said was being used to treat Bryndis. If his mom's research had led to a breakthrough once, maybe it could again . . .

He heard Dr. Hightower's voice in his head. *We've got a team of our top Society scientists working round the clock to try to find an alternative.*

The Synthesis! It was right under his nose. Well, feet, technically.

Throwing on his shoes, Cruz dashed for the door.

"Where you going?" Emmett clicked off the bathroom light.

"Out," said Cruz, yanking on the handle.

The lights flickered, indicating that they had about two minutes before bedtime. "You can't go now," said Emmett.

"Got to," clipped Cruz. "Gotta see Jericho."

"Jericho Miles?" His emoto-glasses turned bright white. "What for?"

"Tell you later." Cruz took off.

"Oh no you don't!" he heard Emmett call after him.

Cruz scurried down the explorers' passage, staying as light on his feet as possible so as not to alert Taryn. He hadn't gotten far when he heard footsteps behind him. It sounded like a galloping horse. Cruz spun to run backward. "Quiet! Do you want to wake the ship?"

"What's . . . going . . . on?" huffed Emmett.

"Can't tell you. A promise is a promise." Cruz backpedaled a few more feet to the end of the corridor, then turned and picked up the pace. Jogging through the atrium, he sped down the steps to the main deck.

Cruz flew around the corner and zipped down another flight to B deck, the lowest deck on the ship.

Rushing past the storage holds, he hoped he'd be able to find the blue door again. Without Bryndis, Hubbard, or Mell here to show him the way, it was going to be tricky. Cruz took his first left, then did his best to navigate the maze of tight corridors from memory. He came to an intersection. Left or right? His gut told him right. His gut was wrong. Hitting a dead end, he had to backtrack. Somewhere along the line, he had lost Emmett, which was just as well. He wouldn't be able to tell Emmett the truth about Bryndis, and that would make Emmett mad—and that would make one more person on board *Orion* angry with him...

The blue door!

Cruz waved his OS band in front of the black security screen that was attached to the wall next to the unmarked door. Like before, when Bryndis had first brought him here, nothing happened. What had he expected? He had no idea. No brilliant plan. Cruz only knew that he was out here and Jericho was in there. He *had* to get into that room! Cruz didn't spot a camera, but that didn't mean one wasn't here. Why, for all he knew, there could be a tiny camera in one of the metal rivets in the wall. He'd seen enough of Fanchon's inventions to know anything was possi—

Fanchon!

She might know someone who could get him in. But she was probably still at the hospital with Bryndis. Cruz looked around. There was only one thing he could think to do. Cruz began to pound on the door.

Boom, boom, boom.

The sound echoed through the deck.

"Hello! Jericho?" shouted Cruz. "Open up! This is an emergency!"

Boom, boom, boom.

Beating his fists against the metal, Cruz felt the vibrations pulse through his body. "Is anyone in there? I need to talk to Jericho! It's about Bryndis. Please, please open the door!"

He kept banging for several minutes, but no one came.

His hands sore, Cruz stopped hammering. He let his head tip forward to rest against the blue door. The metal felt cool against his forehead. Where was everyone? It *had* been a while since Mell had done her surveillance. Could the Synthesis have shut down their secret lab on board *Orion*? Or were Jericho and the pretty dark-haired woman deliberately ignoring him? Cruz watched a bead of sweat fall from his chin. It made a tiny splat on the smooth floor.

"Cruz?" It was Emmett.

"What?" He exhaled the word.

"Bryndis..." He was trying to catch his breath. "... You know ... what's really going on with her ... don't you?"

Cruz was tired. Or maybe he was just tired of keeping secrets. "Yes. Nebula tried to kill me by putting poison in my duffel bag—the one I loaned to Bryndis," he said, his voice barely above a whisper. "I'm the reason she might die."

A hand was on his shoulder. "It's not your fault."

It was the second time Cruz had heard that, but it didn't make it true and it didn't make him feel better.

Another drop of water fell to the floor, and this one wasn't sweat.

Cruz felt a shudder go through his palms. The door—it was moving! Cruz stumbled backward into Emmett. As the blue door slid to one side, a white light from within the room lit up the entire passage. Blinded, Cruz and Emmett shielded their eyes.

A tall figure was coming toward them.

"Fanchon!" rasped Cruz. "You're back."

The tech lab chief slid her safety goggles up over a head scarf covered in butterflies. "Hi, Cruz." She sounded half amused, half annoyed at being discovered.

Someone else came to stand beside Fanchon. Cruz recognized her, too. It was the dark-haired woman Mell had captured on video.

The woman looked from Cruz to his roommate. She let out a sigh. "Hello, Emmett."

Emmett sheepishly pushed his glasses up his nose. "Hi, Mom."

15

"MOM?" rasped Cruz. "I had a feeling that you knew her but...your...MOM?"

Emmett yanked on the crew collar of his pajama tee. "I wanted to tell you, but..."

"Yeah, I know. Top secret."

"Hello, Cruz," said Emmett's mom. "I've heard so much about you. It's a pleasure to finally meet you. I'm Dr. Jilpa Lu." She extended her hand to him.

Cruz numbly took it. "So...you really work for the Syn—"

"Uh-uh." Dr. Lu wagged a finger. "We never use the S-word outside of the lab. In fact, you'll have to go topside, boys. You're not allowed in here." Stepping back, she lifted a hand to a panel in the inside of the door.

"Please," begged Cruz, remembering why he'd come. "I need to talk to you...to someone in the Syn...about Bryndis—"

"I know you're worried." Dr. Lu gave a nervous glance past them. "But I can't let you into the lab, and this is no place for a discussion. Go on up and we'll talk later—"

Cruz put his foot across the doorway. "Sorry. This is too important."

Dr. Lu narrowed her eyes.

Cruz lifted his chin.

Dr. Lu put her hands on her hips.

Cruz lifted his chin higher.

It appeared to be a stalemate.

One tense minute later, Fanchon leaned to say in Dr. Lu's ear, "We could bring them into the DC. No farther."

Dr. Lu didn't blink.

"For a minute," added Fanchon.

"I suppose," said Dr. Lu. "*For a minute.*" She inspected Emmett's pajamas. "Isn't it past your bedtime, young man?"

"Moo-oom."

Dr. Lu motioned for the boys to enter. Cruz put his other leg over the threshold. Emmett stepped in behind him. The blue door closed. About 10 feet ahead was a pair of tinted glass doors. Dr. Lu put up a hand, signaling for the boys to wait while Fanchon and she headed down the passage toward the next set of doors. The two women had their heads together, whispering.

Cruz looked at his roommate. "So that's how you knew so much about the Synthesis. Any other secrets you're keeping from me?"

"Tons," said Emmett, rolling his eyes.

"I can't believe you didn't tell me about your mom," hissed Cruz. He was in no mood for jokes.

"You know the rules," said Emmett. "How was I supposed to tell you that my mom was the director of the Synthesis? Could you tell your friends that your mom worked for a secret scientific agency?"

"No, but this is totally different. You know I'm trying to unravel the mystery surrounding my mother. Maybe your mom and mine worked together. Maybe your mom has some new information. Maybe she could help—"

"She didn't and she doesn't and she can't," snapped Emmett. "If she could have, don't you think I would have told you? My mom only started at the Synthesis a year ago. And trust me, I've asked her a million and one questions about your mom. If you don't believe me, ask her yourself. Ask her anything you want."

Fanchon was motioning for Cruz and Emmett to come to the tinted glass doors. Joining her, Cruz saw that the lights in this small hall were attached to four grids—one on the ceiling, one under a clear floor, and one on each side of the passage. Cruz tried to peer through the dark glass doors that kept them from going farther, but he couldn't see anything other than his own reflection.

"Step inside the black square," directed Fanchon. "Hold still."

Seeing the dark outline beneath him, Cruz moved inside its borders.

The lights surrounding them grew brighter.

Tipping his head, Emmett surveyed the scene. "Ultraviolet light decontamination?"

"I know what you're going to ask," said his mother. "Yes, UV light is invisible to humans, but we need to know when the decontamination process is taking place, so the system is connected to lights in the spectrum we *can* see."

"I knew that, Mom," said Emmett matter-of-factly.

Cruz tugged on Fanchon's candy-cane-striped apron. "About Bryndis—"

"Face forward. Keep still."

"Sorry."

"I know you know the truth about Bryndis," whispered Fanchon out of the side of her mouth. "And *I* know what *you're* going to ask. The answer is yes. We have accessed your mom's files in hopes of finding a new antidote for the toxin that poisoned Bryndis."

"And?"

"It's promising. I'm not at liberty to say more."

He knew it!

"I told you I've read every paper, report, and article your mom ever wrote," said Fanchon. "If something is there, I'll find it."

The main lights shut off, and the perimeter ceiling lights came on, bathing the four of them in a soft bluish purple glow.

"Cruz, we're doing everything we can to help Bryndis," said Dr. Lu. "You have my word on that."

He nodded.

"And now I really should get back to work," said Fanchon. "Every minute I'm away—"

"Go!" cried Cruz.

Fanchon lifted her face to the biometric identification panel. She gazed into it, and a blue beam swept across her eyes. The doors parted, and Fanchon hurried in. Cruz caught only a quick glimpse of a dark room with banks of computer screens before the doors shut again. So close!

Dr. Lu faced them. "Boys, go straight back out the way you came—"

Emmett held up a hand. "Mom, Cruz thinks you might have more details about what happened to his mother. I tried to tell him you didn't, but..."

Her face softened. "Cruz, I wish I could help, but Emmett's right. I don't know any more than what's in the official report, the one your aunt has seen. I *am* sorry. About everything."

"Thanks," said Cruz, his eyes watering.

"Your mother left quite a legacy, Cruz, and if it's any comfort, I intend to make sure it is not only remembered but carried forward."

Cruz could only nod. He didn't want to start crying.

"This has been tough on Emmett." Dr. Lu put a hand on her son's shoulder. "He's had to keep me a big secret from you and everyone at Explorer Academy. But I would never ask him to keep important information about your mother from you. You need to know that."

Cruz gave Emmett an apologetic look. "I guess I already did."

"I must get inside, and the two of you are breaking curfew, so we'd better say good night." Dr. Lu dropped a quick kiss on Emmett's forehead.

"Mom, you'll tell us if Fanchon finds an antidote, won't you?"

"The very second." She moved toward the biometric panel. "Get to bed, Nou-nou."

"Nou-nou?" snorted Cruz as the doors shut behind Emmett's mom.

Emmett shot him a sideways glare. "That's one secret I'm keeping."

"TARYN TO ALL EXPLORERS!" Startled at the voice coming through the comm pin he was trying to attach to his uniform, Cruz poked the tack straight into his thumb. Cruz and Emmett had overslept. They had only a few minutes to get to first period.

"Please report to the conference room instead of first period this morning," said their adviser. "All explorers to the conference room at eight a.m. for a brief but urgent meeting."

Urgent?

Sucking the drop of blood that had appeared on the tip of his thumb, Cruz froze. Taryn had told them she would gather the explorers when she had more news about Bryndis.

Emmett looked up from putting on his shoes. "Do you think—"

"Let's get up there." Several pinpricks later, he finally succeeded in putting on his comm, GPS, and shadow badges. He could add Mell's remote later, once she was home.

It had become customary for the explorers to sit with their respective teams whenever Taryn called them to a meeting. Today was no exception. Entering the conference room, Emmett and Cruz took their usual seats next to Sailor and Dugan on the left side of the table. The four of them stared at the empty chair between Sailor and Dugan. They weren't the only ones. Other explorers were sneaking looks at Bryndis's chair, too. When Lani came in, Cruz grabbed another chair from the back wall and rolled it up to the table for her. Six explorers on Team Cousteau. Six chairs. That's how it was meant to be.

"Your comm pin is upside down," Lani whispered to Cruz. She reached out, spinning the EA logo right side up. Lani's eyes locked on to his. Neither of them wanted to say what they were both thinking: that they were here for Bryndis.

Sailor looked absolutely terrified. Cruz covered her hand with his.

At precisely 8:00, Taryn and Professor Ishikawa strolled purposefully into the room.

"Good morning," said Taryn seriously.

"Good morning," most of them answered. Cruz opened his mouth, but nothing came out.

"Professor Ishikawa has some news to share, and then you are to report directly to Manatee classroom," said Taryn. "Dr. Gabriel is expecting you ten minutes late."

"I'll get right to the point." Professor Ishikawa clasped his hands. "I spoke with Dr. Najjemba this morning. He tells me that since our mission both groups of gorillas at Bwindi are showing signs of significant improvement. They are no longer presenting symptoms of the virus—"

"Even the baby?" blurted Shristine.

"Even the baby." Their teacher grinned. "The veterinary team will be continuing to monitor the situation, of course, but all signs seem to indicate that our mission was a success. Well done, explorers."

The students exploded from their chairs. They whooped. They clapped. They hugged. Cruz threw his arms around Lani—glad for the gorillas, but equally as happy that it wasn't bad news about Bryndis. Cruz found Shristine and Felipe and congratulated them. He looked for Ali, too, but he was on the other side of the room.

Taryn whistled. "All right, people, first period awaits!"

Cruz was determined to talk to Ali before the day was out. Two hours later, as the explorers assembled in the CAVE for fitness and survival training, he saw his chance. Monsieur Legrand usually had them line up along one wall so they could stretch before doing whatever activity he had planned for the day. Today, only a few lights in the large compartment that housed the CAVE were on. They could see nothing beyond a few feet from inside the entrance, so they remained close to the wall.

When Cruz saw Ali walk in with Dugan, he started toward them.

"*Bonjour, explorateurs.*" Monsieur Legrand emerged from the darkness, his long legs striding across the floor. "Let's get warmed up. Line up in your teams for jumping jacks. *Veuillez commencer!*"

Cruz backpedaled into his usual spot between Emmett and Sailor to begin their set of synchronized exercises.

Dugan hurried to join them. "I wonder what we're doing. I hope it's snowboarding."

"I hope it's river rafting," countered Sailor.

"BASE jumping," huffed Cruz.

"Sepak takraw," said Emmett.

"Gesundheit," teased Sailor.

"I didn't sneeze, Sailor. Sepak takraw is the Malaysian sport of—"

"Kick volleyball," finished Lani. "And I'm crossing my fingers for surfing."

"Surfing!" cried Dugan. "I change my vote. I'm with Lani."

As it turned out, it was none of those things. "We're playing a game!" announced Monsieur Legrand, earning a round of applause. In one hand, he gently tossed a black ball with red stripes that was slightly smaller than a soccer ball. "It's called Talustrike."

Cruz had never heard of it. He glanced at Sailor, who lifted a shoulder. Emmett shook his head. Everyone else looked confused as well. That's when Cruz caught the smirk on their instructor's face.

Emmett had seen it, too. "A Legrand original," he muttered. "Prepare to be unprepared."

"*Lumières,*" ordered Monsieur Legrand, and the overhead lights in the compartment came up, revealing an oval arena more than twice the width and length of a basketball court. A rocky outcrop rose from each end of the court like a pair of bookends, stretching to the top of the CAVE's 20-foot ceiling. Each cliff had stairs cut into the left and right sides. Some of the steps wound behind sharp spikes of craggy rock, while others were completely exposed with nothing between them and a long drop to the court below. Several vines trailed from ceiling to floor on the outer edges of the bluffs. About two-thirds of the way up each bluff was a large hole. Cruz estimated the opening to be about four feet wide by four feet high. Was that the goal?

"The idea is to throw *this* ball through *that* opening." Their instructor pointed to the gaping hole high in the rock. "You only get one shot per offensive run and no rebounds. There are several ways to score. You can shoot from where you are standing on the gaming surface, but it's about a fifteen-foot shot. You can take the steps on either side of the cliff to get closer. You can also use the kelp."

"Kelp? You mean seaweed?" groaned Sailor. "Isn't that kind of slippery?"

"We can do it," said Cruz. "Get a good run down the hardcourt and jump on."

"Uh, Cruz?" Dugan frowned. "I don't think that's a wood court."

Cruz craned his neck. "What is it?"

"*Le sable!*" proclaimed Monsieur Legrand. "Sand!"

"Whoa!" cried Cruz, along with the other explorers.

Monsieur Legrand gave them all the rules. Two teams would play, five-on-five for two seven-minute halves (since Bryndis wasn't here, one player on each of the other three teams would sit out). The object of the game was to race down the sand to the opponent's cliff, passing the ball between teammates with your hands without dropping it, while the other team tried to intercept it. Stealing was made easier by the fact that no one player could hold the ball for more than four seconds. If you did, a buzzer inside the ball would sound. Monsieur Legrand, who was the referee, would then hand the ball over to the other team. It was true—there were lots of ways to score, but Cruz quickly saw that none of those ways were easy. If you tried shooting long-distance from the sand, you'd be lucky to hit the opening. On the other hand, if you raced up the steps or swung in on the kelp, and an opposing player found a faster way to get there, he or she could easily block you from ever shooting at all.

"I've selected the matchups," said Monsieur Legrand. "Team Galileo, you'll play Team Earhart. Team Magellan, you'll go up against Team

Cousteau. The winners of both matches will play for the championship. Cousteau and Magellan, you're up first." He pointed to a neat row of helmets on the outer edge of the court. Half of the helmets were purple. Half were green. "Cousteau take the purple. Magellan, you're green," said Monsieur Legrand, easily vaulting over the four-foot retaining wall to land softly on the sand.

Everyone grabbed their helmets. The moment Cruz stepped onto the sand, he sunk in up to his ankles. He had to throw his arm out to keep from falling.

"What is this, quicksand?" cried Emmett, whose feet had also disappeared.

Cruz had a feeling he knew why the sand was so deep. This way, no one would be tempted to kick the ball.

Monsieur Legrand directed them to line up in a circle around him, as they would do if they were playing basketball. Kat, Matteo, Tao, Yulia, and Ali (Zane was sitting out) made up one semicircle, and Cruz, Emmett, Sailor, Lani, and Dugan formed the other.

"Dugan should take the tip-off," suggested Cruz. "He's the tallest."

His teammates agreed.

Kat stepped forward as the center for her team.

Ali lined up across from Cruz. As Cruz got into his stance, their eyes met. Was it the lights, or was Ali glaring at him? Cruz broke their gaze to look up at the ball perched on his teacher's fingertips.

"Talustrike program, level one, begin," said their teacher. "Oh, and, explorers," he boomed so all the teams could hear, "there's one more thing."

"Wuh-oh," whispered Emmett. "Here it comes."

"As you play"—Monsieur Legrand raised an eyebrow—"try not to step on the scorpions."

16

"SCORPIONS!" squealed Dugan, frantically searching the sand around him. "*Where?*"

"Easy, Dugan, they're not real." Monsieur Legrand chuckled. "However, you will feel a small jab on your leg or ankle so you know you've been stung. If stung, you must stop where you are for a half minute before getting back into the game. The light inside your helmet will turn from red to green once the thirty seconds are up. Also, if you're holding the ball when the scorpion strikes, play stops, and the ball goes over to the other team. Any questions?"

Sailor raised a hand. "Let me see if I've got this: slippery seaweed, scary cliffs, high steps, *and* deadly arachnids?"

"*Oui,*" said Monsieur Legrand proudly.

Sailor threw her head back. "And I wanted to be an explorer."

With the tweet of Monsieur Legrand's whistle, their teacher tossed the black ball in the air. Dugan's fingertips tapped it to Lani. She swung out wide to the right, took four steps, and whipped the ball to Sailor, who was next to

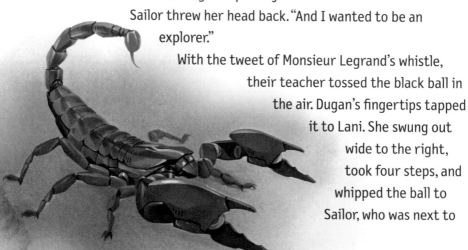

her on the inside. Cruz was out on the far-left wing. He was trying to keep up with his teammates, but it was like running in pudding. The sand was dragging him down. Every step was an effort. He'd barely gone 30 feet, and he was already out of breath. Sailor flung the ball to Emmett, who put a nice stop-and-go move on Matteo to speed past him.

With no one guarding him, Cruz made a break for the stairs on his side of the cliff. He took the steps two at a time—not easy considering they were all different sizes. As Cruz neared the goal, the shorter spikes on the outer rim gave him a good view of play below. He saw Lani hurl the ball to Dugan. No one from Team Magellan was climbing the cliff. The goal was clear.

"Dugan!" shouted Cruz.

Yulia was backing Dugan into the far-left corner.

"Here, Dugan!" yelled Cruz. "Above you."

Dugan was trying to go around Yulia. He had to have heard Cruz calling for the ball. Was he going to take the shot himself? From that sharp angle and distance, he'd never make it.

"Dugan!" Lani chimed in when she saw Cruz on the bluff. "Throw it up to—"

Bzzzzzzz!

Dugan had held the ball too long. Cruz dropped his arms. However, there was no time to sulk. Matteo was already inbounding. Cruz joined the players sprinting down the sandy court. He discovered if he took quick, light steps and followed the footprints of, well, *anyone*, he wouldn't sink quite as far. Racing ahead of her team, Tao was trying to climb a thick strand of kelp. Yulia, Kat, Matteo, and Ali were passing the ball between them with Team Cousteau on defense.

Suddenly, a pair of dark pincers popped out of the sand between Cruz's feet. He turned his ankle, barely missing the C-shaped tail of a black scorpion. That was close! Ali was running up the cliff on the opposite side of Tao with Sailor in pursuit.

"I'll protect the goal," cried Cruz to his team, taking off for the steps near Tao.

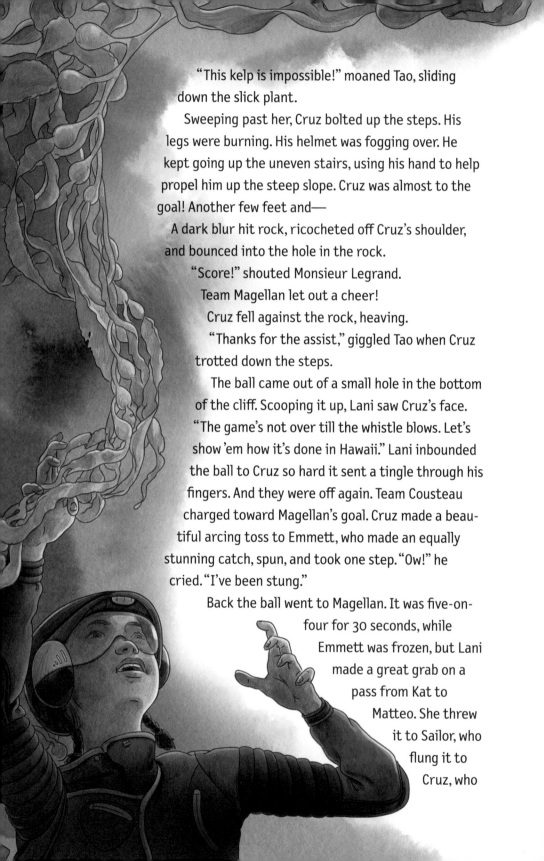

"This kelp is impossible!" moaned Tao, sliding down the slick plant.

Sweeping past her, Cruz bolted up the steps. His legs were burning. His helmet was fogging over. He kept going up the uneven stairs, using his hand to help propel him up the steep slope. Cruz was almost to the goal! Another few feet and—

A dark blur hit rock, ricocheted off Cruz's shoulder, and bounced into the hole in the rock.

"Score!" shouted Monsieur Legrand.

Team Magellan let out a cheer!

Cruz fell against the rock, heaving.

"Thanks for the assist," giggled Tao when Cruz trotted down the steps.

The ball came out of a small hole in the bottom of the cliff. Scooping it up, Lani saw Cruz's face. "The game's not over till the whistle blows. Let's show 'em how it's done in Hawaii." Lani inbounded the ball to Cruz so hard it sent a tingle through his fingers. And they were off again. Team Cousteau charged toward Magellan's goal. Cruz made a beautiful arcing toss to Emmett, who made an equally stunning catch, spun, and took one step. "Ow!" he cried. "I've been stung."

Back the ball went to Magellan. It was five-on-four for 30 seconds, while Emmett was frozen, but Lani made a great grab on a pass from Kat to Matteo. She threw it to Sailor, who flung it to Cruz, who tossed it to Dugan, who took a shot that hit the wall a good five feet below the target. Cruz stifled a groan. For the next five minutes, the teams went back and forth running, passing, shooting, stealing, and occasionally getting stung by the pop-up scorpions. However, no one scored. The first half ended with Magellan ahead 1–0.

"Two-minute water and rest break," called Monsieur Legrand.

"Huddle up," said Sailor, motioning for the team to gather round. "We need a plan."

"As long as it doesn't involve seaweed." Emmett pulled off his helmet. His hair was matted to his skull. "Did you see how much trouble Tao had trying to climb that slippery thing?"

"Agreed," said Sailor. "Avoid the kelp."

"How about a fake-out?" offered Emmett. "Four of us go right, and the fifth takes off for the left stairs."

"Or a fake-out fake-out," said Cruz. "We pretend to do that, but instead, we protect the right stairs and one of the four of us goes up those. By the time Magellan figures it out—"

"It'll be too late," said Sailor.

"I'll be the decoy to the left," said Emmett.

"I'll be the shooter," said Dugan.

"No!" shouted the rest of the team.

"Let's give it to Lani," suggested Sailor. "She's fast."

"At least I didn't score for the other team," grumbled Dugan.

"He didn't do it on purpose," scolded Lani. "We're a team. We stick together. Good shots or bad."

"Sorry," said Dugan, surprising Cruz. He had expected a biting comeback.

Dugan won the tip-off and flicked the ball to Cruz, who whipped it out wide to Emmett. His roommate threw it to Dugan, then zigzagged for the left corner near the base of the cliff. Matteo took the bait and followed. The rest of Team Cousteau veered right with the remaining members of Magellan on their tails.

"*Foi mal!*" yelped Yulia. She'd been stung.

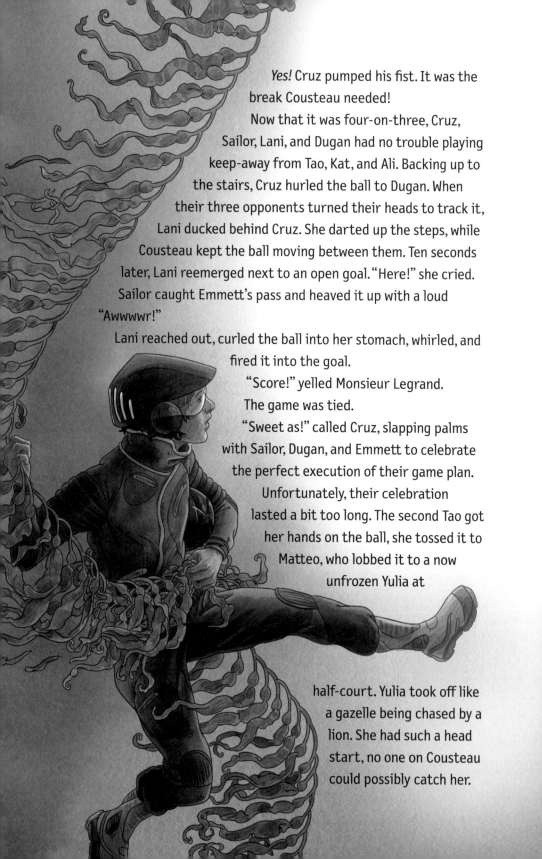

Yes! Cruz pumped his fist. It was the break Cousteau needed!

Now that it was four-on-three, Cruz, Sailor, Lani, and Dugan had no trouble playing keep-away from Tao, Kat, and Ali. Backing up to the stairs, Cruz hurled the ball to Dugan. When their three opponents turned their heads to track it, Lani ducked behind Cruz. She darted up the steps, while Cousteau kept the ball moving between them. Ten seconds later, Lani reemerged next to an open goal. "Here!" she cried.

Sailor caught Emmett's pass and heaved it up with a loud "Awwwwr!"

Lani reached out, curled the ball into her stomach, whirled, and fired it into the goal.

"Score!" yelled Monsieur Legrand.

The game was tied.

"Sweet as!" called Cruz, slapping palms with Sailor, Dugan, and Emmett to celebrate the perfect execution of their game plan. Unfortunately, their celebration lasted a bit too long. The second Tao got her hands on the ball, she tossed it to Matteo, who lobbed it to a now unfrozen Yulia at half-court. Yulia took off like a gazelle being chased by a lion. She had such a head start, no one on Cousteau could possibly catch her.

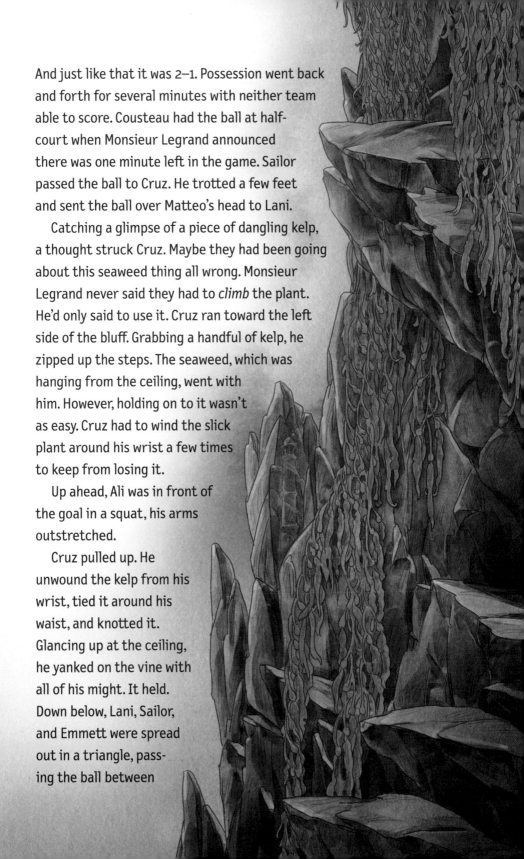

And just like that it was 2–1. Possession went back and forth for several minutes with neither team able to score. Cousteau had the ball at half-court when Monsieur Legrand announced there was one minute left in the game. Sailor passed the ball to Cruz. He trotted a few feet and sent the ball over Matteo's head to Lani.

Catching a glimpse of a piece of dangling kelp, a thought struck Cruz. Maybe they had been going about this seaweed thing all wrong. Monsieur Legrand never said they had to *climb* the plant. He'd only said to use it. Cruz ran toward the left side of the bluff. Grabbing a handful of kelp, he zipped up the steps. The seaweed, which was hanging from the ceiling, went with him. However, holding on to it wasn't as easy. Cruz had to wind the slick plant around his wrist a few times to keep from losing it.

Up ahead, Ali was in front of the goal in a squat, his arms outstretched.

Cruz pulled up. He unwound the kelp from his wrist, tied it around his waist, and knotted it. Glancing up at the ceiling, he yanked on the vine with all of his might. It held. Down below, Lani, Sailor, and Emmett were spread out in a triangle, pass-ing the ball between them as they looked for a chance to score.

Cruz cupped his hands around his mouth. "Up here!"

Lani, who had the ball, glanced up. She launched it toward him.

All eyes were fixed on the black orb soaring through the air. Cruz saw that it was curving toward the center of the cliff. He ran toward it and, throwing out his arms, caught the ball. Cruz pulled it into his chest. But he didn't stop running. Instead, he went faster, shifting things until the vine was in his right hand and the ball was cradled between his left forearm and body. With one last look over the rim, Cruz swung wide and stepped right off the edge of the cliff!

Someone screamed. It sounded like Sailor, but he couldn't tell because...

He was flying!

The seaweed held. Cruz's run had given him plenty of momentum to keep moving forward, as he'd hoped. As he swung, Cruz got ready to toss the ball into the goal. He'd have to time it right to avoid Ali.

"Oh no you don't," growled Ali. "You're not going to be a hero hog this time..."

All Cruz had to do was lob the ball past Ali's head. A couple more seconds and he'd be there...

Ali was lunging straight for Cruz. If he wasn't careful, he was going to go right off the edge of the cliff! Cruz did not take his eyes off the opening in the rock. Al-most there.

Three ... two ... one ...

Now!

The moment Cruz released the ball, he felt a sharp pain in his side. He was still flying, but his seaweed rope was now spinning. He could feel his grip starting to go, too.

Hang on, hang on!

He wasn't sure if he was thinking it or someone was yelling it. Everything was whirling and whizzing past. Cruz's hip bumped the side of the cliff. Suddenly, the sand was rising up to meet him. Cruz smashed into the ground. Hard. Pain pierced both ankles. The wind knocked from his lungs, he could only lie on the sand, gasping.

His teacher's face hovered over him. "Cruz, are you okay?"

"Yeah," rasped Cruz. "Did I . . . score?"

Sailor peered down at him. "I told you to avoid the kelp."

"But . . . did I score?"

Lani ripped off her helmet. "It's okay," she said. "You tried."

Her meaning was clear. He had not scored.

The game was over. Magellan had won. They would advance to the final.

Once he was able to breathe normally again, Cruz sat up. He took off his helmet. Emmett and Dugan helped him to his feet, and Cruz limped off the court with his team. Teams Earhart and Galileo clapped when they saw he was all right and jogged out to play their match. Team Magellan had already retreated to the far corner of the CAVE to plan a strategy for the final.

"Uh . . . Cruz, you're bleeding," said Lani.

Cruz saw a splotch of red about the size of half a candy bar near his waist. He lifted his shirt to see three short but deep scratches. Ali's fingernails, no doubt.

"Oooo!" said Sailor. "Do you want to go to sick bay?"

"No," answered Cruz. "I'll go get cleaned up and be right back."

Cruz headed for the boys' bathroom not far down the passage. Once inside, Cruz leaned against the sink. Had Ali hurt him on purpose? Or had he merely gotten carried away with the game? He'd never forget the sneer on Ali's face or the way he'd yelled at him. Cruz pulled up his shirt. "Geez, Ali. I didn't know you could be so mean."

Glancing up, Cruz saw a reflection in the mirror that wasn't his. "Dugan! I . . . I . . . I didn't hear you . . ."

"Thought you could use a hand. It's hard to put a bandage on yourself."

"Thanks."

While Dugan got the first aid kit out of the cabinet beside the sink, Cruz splashed cold water on his face. He patted it dry with a paper towel.

"Bad cut," said Dugan, popping open the kit.

Holding his shirt up, Cruz looked at the ceiling. "Must have ... uh ... caught one of those spikes going down."

"A three-pronged spike, huh?" Dugan grunted. "Bleeding's stopped. I want to clean it, so this is going to—"

"Owwww!" Cruz's waist was on fire. Tears sprang to his eyes.

"Sting," said Dugan.

The pain easing, Cruz felt a slight pressure. Dugan was applying the bandage.

"Done," pronounced Dugan. "I think you'll live."

"That's what my dad always says."

While Dugan washed his hands, Cruz put the first aid kit away.

"Thanks again, Dugan," said Cruz as the pair headed back to the CAVE.

"No problem. I owed you. You know, from orientation."

Cruz had almost forgotten about their first day at the Academy, how he'd gone back for Dugan, who had stubbornly refused to follow the clues Dr. Hightower had left so they could find her in the CAVE. That day seemed ages and ages ago.

"You don't owe me," said Cruz. "We're teammates ... and friends."

He wasn't totally sure about the friends part. It had sort of ... popped out. Even though he might not have intended it, Cruz was glad he'd said it, 'cause the kid who never smiled finally did.

17

"DO YOU KNOW what scares an elephant?" asked Cruz, gazing out at his audience.

"Losing his trunk at the airport?" burst Felipe.

Everyone laughed, even Professor Gabriel.

"Close, but no," said Cruz. "It's bees!" Cruz was wrapping up his presentation on a conservation plan for an endangered African animal.

"African elephants have an instinctive fear of bees, so conservationists decided to try spraying bee pheromones near farmlands. The idea was to prevent migrating elephants from trampling the farmers' crops. And it worked!"

Along with discussing how to avoid human-elephant conflicts, Cruz also shared some of the other threats to elephants, including poaching. Hunters killed elephants to provide tusks for the ivory trade. Ivory was against the law in most countries, but that did not stop poachers.

"Elephants are intelligent and emotional," concluded Cruz. "They teach their young. They mourn their dead. They learn and remember the best spots to eat and drink. And if we don't protect them, we're going to lose them." As Cruz took his seat, the class applauded.

"Thank you, Cruz," said Professor Gabriel. He glanced down at his computer screen. "Let's see who's next... Dugan, let's hear your conservation plan for the cheetah."

Dugan headed to the front of the class.

"Nice job," Lani whispered to Cruz. "I always thought it was a myth about elephants having good memories."

"Not at all," said Cruz. "I read an article about two elephants that recognized each other after being apart for twenty years."

"Really? I bet elephants don't change much in twenty years. Not like people. I can't even imagine what I'll look like when I'm thirty-two."

Cruz gave her a sideways grin. "I'll still recognize you."

Lani tugged on the silver streak in her hair. "I'm keeping this, just to be sure. By then it'll probably be naturally gray, like my mom's. Ugh. Forty is *so* old."

"Don't tell her I told you…" Cruz leaned in. "Aunt Marisol is forty-two!"

They had to stop talking. Professor Gabriel was glaring at them over the rims of his glasses. Dugan was going over some cheetah facts, as he showed a holo-video of the powerful cat speeding through the savanna. "Cheetahs are the fastest animal on land," said Dugan. "They can go from zero to seventy miles per hour in three seconds. They have long, muscular, flat tails that help them balance and steer, kind of like the rudder on a boat…"

The mail icon on Cruz's tablet was blinking. It was against the rules to check mail during class. After watching it flash for several minutes, Cruz slid the computer into his lap. He tapped the icon with his pinkie. It was a message from Aunt Marisol.

> **Cruz,**
> **I've got a lead on your clue! Years ago, your**
> **mom worked on a**

Chirp! Chirp!

Cruz's head popped up. He knew that sound! At first, he thought it was coming from his tablet, that somehow he'd accidentally hit the play button on the video of the cryptogram.

Chirp!

Cruz froze. The noise was not coming from his computer.

"...cheetahs can't roar," Dugan was explaining to the class. "They need a special bone in their throat to roar. Instead, they make a noise like a bird tweet. It's called a chirp or chirrup. Chirrups can be heard from up to a mile away."

Chirp!

Watching a mother cheetah chirping to her cubs, Cruz nearly fell out of his chair. He wasn't the only one freaking out. Emmett's emoto-glasses were a carousel of yellows, greens, and pinks. Lani's mouth was open wide. On the other side of Lani, Sailor was leaning forward. They all knew, too!

"Cheetahs make other noises," added Dugan. "They purr, hiss, growl..."

Emmett was elbowing Cruz. "There's only one place on Earth where cheetahs still roam free."

Cruz knew: Namibia.

"There's a cheetah center there," said Emmett. "I'm certain of it."

"Me too," whispered Cruz. He'd finished reading Aunt Marisol's message. Cruz turned the screen so his roommate could see it, too.

Cruz,

I've got a lead on your clue! Years ago, your mom worked on a research program at the Namibia Center for Cheetah Conservation. She became friends with the woman who now runs it, Dr. Ziyanda Jojozi. I contacted Dr. Jo, and she says she has been long looking forward to meeting YOU—knew your name, too! I think we're hot on the trail! We dock in Mombasa soon, so I will have to work quickly to arrange things.

Love,
Aunt Marisol

P.S. I hope you read chapter six in your text— unit quiz on archaeology ethics today!

CRUZ FOLDED HIS FOREARMS, one over the other, on the rail of his veranda. He lifted his chin to the afternoon sun, letting the brisk wind cool his face. *Orion* was slicing through the dark blue waters of the Indian Ocean, beginning her turn toward the channel leading into the Port of Mombasa. Beside him, Emmett had tapped his GPS pin and was reading the information it was projecting over a back-drop of rocky coastline. "We're heading for Kilindini Harbor," said Emmett. "Kilindini is a Swahili word that means 'deep.' The harbor is up to a hundred and eighty feet deep at the center."

"Uh-huh," said Cruz as the ship smoothly sailed by a black-and-white-striped lighthouse guarding the point. The leaves on a line of palm trees swayed, as if to welcome them.

"Mombasa is one of Kenya's oldest cities. It was once a key trading port for gold, ivory, and spices..." Emmett was still rattling on, but Cruz had stopped listening.

He had his eye on a windsurfer. Seeing the billowing white sail cut behind the stern of the ship to ride its wake, Cruz felt a twinge of envy.

How was it that he spent so much time on the water but hardly any time in it? Besides his dad, that's what Cruz missed most about home. The comforting way the foamy water swirled around his ankles as he ran into the surf, how the sea gently rocked on his board as he waited for the swell of a good wave, even when a monster curl punished him for losing his balance—Cruz loved everything about the water. Leaning back, the surfer shifted the angle of his mast and skipped out of *Orion*'s wake. Cruz stretched out over the rail as far as he could, watching until the surfer disappeared around the side of the ship. Cruz wished he could kitesurf or windsurf, but he knew they would not be staying long in Mombasa.

Before school had let out, Professor Gabriel had come into Professor Benedict's journalism class. He was carrying a small black velvet pouch. "Explorers, there's been a slight change in our expedition plans. We've had a special request from one of the Society's most dedicated scientists. I am pleased to share that Dr. Jojozi of the Namibia Center for Cheetah Conservation learned about our SHOT-bot program and has invited you to deploy them near Waterberg Plateau Park."

Cruz smacked his fist against the side of his desk. *Thank you, Aunt Marisol!*

"Given this exciting development," their conservation teacher continued, "half of you will come with Professor Ishikawa and me to Tanzania, as planned. The other half will go to Namibia with Professor Coronado and Dr. Vanderwick."

Cruz edged forward in his seat. It wasn't a done deal quite yet, not until he heard the actual words…

"Since Dugan gave such an excellent presentation on cheetah conservation," said Professor Gabriel, "Cousteau will be one of the Namibia teams."

And thank you, Dugan!

"We're going to draw for the other Namibia team." Their conservation teacher held out the velvet pouch to Professor Benedict. "Will you do the honors?"

Rubbing her hands together, she dipped one into the bag. Cruz watched her mix up the three chips he knew were inside. Grinning, she pulled one out. The room was deathly still. She turned the chip over. "Galileo!"

Cruz relaxed. He wouldn't have to worry about Ali. Plus, Felipe and Misha were the only members of Team Galileo that he'd spent much time around. It would be nice to get to know Blessica, Corazón, Weatherly, and Pashelle better. Blessica was the only American (she was from Brooklyn, New York). Pashelle was Greek, Weatherly was English, Cory was Mexican, Felipe was Chilean, and Misha was a Turkmen (he'd explained back at the Academy that Turkmen was the term for a citizen of Turkmenistan).

A tug on his sleeve brought Cruz back to the rail of *Orion*. "We'd better get ready," Emmett was saying. "We'll be docking soon."

They went inside their cabin.

Taryn had let Cruz borrow her duffel until his new one arrived. He double-checked its contents, making sure he'd packed everything he thought he might need for the next couple of days. Emmett was doing the same thing. Looking at his friend, Cruz did a double take. Was that a red line on Emmett's OS band? Cruz stepped around his bed, tilting his head for a closer look at his roommate's wrist. He saw the word "cardio."

"Uh . . . Em?"

"Yeah?" He was zipping up a side pocket.

"Either you're dead or the heart monitor on your OS band is malfunctioning."

Emmett turned his arm. "Oh. Yeah." He didn't seem too concerned that he was flatlining. "It's my mom. It means she needs to talk to me."

"You'd better fix it, 'cause knowing Taryn—any second she'll come barging in here with a defibrillator and yell, 'Clear!'"

Emmett laughed. "Nah. We know how to bypass Taryn's computer."

Why didn't that surprise him?

"So shouldn't you . . . uh . . . answer your signal?" urged Cruz.

"You mean, here? Now?"

"Why not?"

"I … uh, I guess I could. I'm used to going to the refrigeration hold on B deck, which is usually pretty cold, or up to the greenhouse on the obs deck, which is usually pretty hot."

"Well, Goldilocks, now you've got someplace that's just right."

Pushing his lime glasses up his nose, Emmett came back to sit on his bed. "It's going to feel strange, talking to her in front of you."

"Want me to leave?"

"No." Emmett smacked his comm pin. "Emmett Lu to Jilpa Lu."

"Hi, Emmett," said his mother a second later. "I've got news."

A tsunami of goose bumps washed over Cruz.

He heard Emmett swallow. "Yeah?"

"Fanchon had a breakthrough," said Dr. Lu. "Looks like she's found an antidote. It's based on Petra Coronado's research."

Standing at the end of his bed, Cruz fell backward onto it. *Yes!*

"We shipped it by rapid drone to Kampala. It should arrive in less than an hour. We're not out of the woods yet," cautioned Dr. Lu. "We'll know more in the next thirty-six hours or so."

"Thanks, Mom," said Emmett. "Keep me posted."

"I will. I hear you're off to Namibia. Don't forget to wear sunscreen."

"I won't."

"And take your hat—the one with the neck flap because you know how easily you burn."

Emmett rolled his eyes at Cruz. "I will."

"I almost forgot. I sent Fanchon to get some rest, but before she left, she asked me to do her a small favor. It should be arriving any minute now. Jilpa Lu, out."

Turning, Cruz went up on one elbow. "Arriving?"

Emmett's eyebrows went up.

The boys waited for a knock at the door.

When it didn't come, Cruz collapsed onto his back once again. He let his head sink into his pillow.

Bzzzzzz!

Two gold eyes were flashing at him.

"Mell!" Cruz bolted up, smacking his forehead into the MAV. The little drone tumbled into his lap. "Oh no!" Ten seconds back and he had broken her already?

"Mell, I'm sorry," said Cruz, gently turning her over. She didn't look damaged, but there was only one way to know for sure. "Mell, test flight."

Flashing her eyes twice to signal she understood, the bee rose to eye level. She hovered there for five seconds, then flitted off on a figure-eight course that took her to every corner of the cabin. They watched her zip to within an inch of the ceiling, then go into a steep dive toward the floor, swooping upward in the nick of time. Fanchon wasn't kidding. She *had* made Mell better! The drone was definitely faster, and her turns were more precise. Banking around Emmett, who was still sitting on his bed, Mell headed for the porthole. This always made Cruz nervous. He was sure she was going to smack into the window. He slapped a hand over his eyes, peering out between his second and third fingers until she had safely completed the turn. Mell took another dip leading into an impressive barrel roll before finally returning to Cruz's outstretched hand. Pulling up, she made a perfect landing, tickling the center of his palm.

"Show-off," said Cruz as she touched down.

Mell tipped her head.

Hooooooonk!

It was *Orion*'s horn. They could feel the ship slowing. It was time to go.

Still holding his MAV, Cruz shoved his arms into his jacket. He opened his fist. "Mell, off." When her gold eyes went dark, Cruz carefully tucked her in the upper-right pocket of his jacket.

Emmett led the way. Cruz was halfway out the door before he realized he'd forgotten one crucial item. "Mell's remote!" He spun. "You go on, Emmett, I'll be right behind you." Cruz scurried to his nightstand. He flipped the lid off the white box and grabbed the only pin left inside. As he lifted it, a piece of the cotton bedding stuck to the honeycomb. Cruz shook it free. He was attaching the remote to his uniform when, through a cloudy haze of cotton, two words on the bottom of the inside of the box caught his attention.

Spy. Danger.

"Emmett Lu to Cruz Coronado."

Cruz hit his comm pin. "Cruz, here."

"You coming? They're lowering the gangway."

"One sec." Cruz flipped the box and shook it. The rest of the fluffy cotton drifted out. Turning his palm right side up he read the message written inside the container:

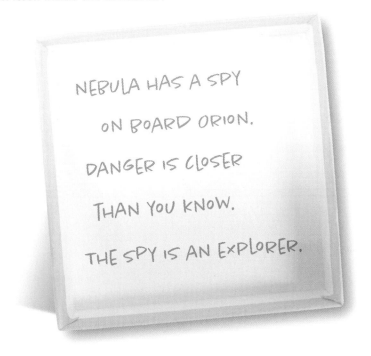

NEBULA HAS A SPY

ON BOARD ORION.

DANGER IS CLOSER

THAN YOU KNOW.

THE SPY IS AN EXPLORER.

18

WATERBERG PLATEAU, NAMIBIA

ANGOLA ZAMBIA
ZIMBABWE
MOZAMBIQUE
BOTSWANA
NAMIBIA
ESWATINI
Atlantic Ocean
SOUTH AFRICA LESOTHO
Indian Ocean

▶ **"THERE IT IS!"** Emmett lurched forward, smacking his shoulder on the dash of the autonomous four-by-four. "The Waterberg Plateau!"

Dr. Vanderwick, seated next to Emmett, and Cruz, Sailor, Lani, and Dugan, who were in the back two rows, uttered the same word at the same time: "Wow!"

A majestic flat-topped mountain rose from the flatlands like a vast stone city. Wrapped in a dense base of bright green bushes and trees, the sandstone fortress glowed scarlet in the midday sun. Cruz, sitting behind Emmett, turned toward the window so his GPS sunglasses could identify the landscape:

-20.416667°S, 17.216667°E
650-FOOT-TALL TABLETOP MOUNTAIN

At 30 miles long and nearly 10 miles wide, the Waterberg Plateau was established as a sanctuary during a time of war in the 1970s. Conservationists rescued animals such as black rhinos, sable antelopes, elands, and African buffalo from other embattled wildlife preserves and transported them to the high bluffs. The 650-foot-tall tabletop mountain provided the protection the animals needed to keep them safe from war, hunters, and other threats. Today, the plateau and 156 square miles surrounding it make up Waterberg Plateau Park. The park is home to a number of animals at risk, such as the white rhino, black rhino, cheetah, and leopard, along with hundreds of other species, including baboons, antelopes, zebras, giraffes, and more than 200 kinds of birds.

The vehicle was slowing. Cruz hoped that they were close to their destination. It seemed like they had been traveling forever. Yesterday's plane ride from Mombasa to Windhoek, Namibia's capital, had taken about four hours. They'd arrived late in the evening and, after a breakfast of scrambled eggs, tomatoes, and sausage, had gotten an early start for Waterberg.

The cheetah conservation center was almost 200 miles north of the capital. They'd been on the road for nearly five hours, driving through the flat scrublands on a dust-blown, pencil-straight road. In Namibia, cars drive on the left side. It made Cruz feel weird, like trying to write with your left hand when you were right-handed. They'd had to break once for an oryx leaping across the road; twice to charge the vehicle, which was having trouble holding a charge; and three times for Emmett, who also was having trouble holding a charge.

"How can he possibly eat so much, so often?" asked Lani as they stretched their legs at a charging station and watched Emmett dig into a container of papaya yogurt.

"He's part pygmy shrew," kidded Sailor. "They have to eat almost constantly or they'll die."

"I have a fast metabolism." Emmett licked his spoon. "What can I say?"

The long drive had also given Cruz time to think. Was the anonymous message true? Or was it from Nebula, who was trying to scare him? Lowering his sunglasses, Cruz let his gaze wander from the back of Emmett's head to a drowsing Sailor next to him, then to Lani and Dugan sitting behind him.

Danger is closer than you know.

Could the spy be one of his teammates? Even a trusted friend?

The Auto Auto was turning off the highway. Bouncing down a dirt road, the four-wheel drive sent up such a big dust cloud Cruz almost missed the sign: EGUMBO GUEST HOUSE. He stifled a groan. He'd hoped they would be going straight to the research center. It was already past one o'clock. Would he have to wait until tomorrow's mission to meet Dr. Jojozi?

Their car came to a stop next to an identical vehicle. It was no doubt the one that had brought Aunt Marisol and Team Galileo.

"I bet Galileo's unpacked, had lunch, and deployed all the SHOT-bots by now," snorted Dugan.

"Impossible," said Dr. Vanderwick. "We brought the bots."

That got a cheer from Team Cousteau.

"You have arrived at your destination," said the female voice of the onboard computer. "The current temperature is eighty-one degrees

under partly sunny skies. Thunderstorms are expected this afternoon with a high of eighty-eight. This vehicle is programmed to remain here for your use for the next three days. To extend your time or if you require assistance, please press the help button. We hope you have enjoyed your ride. Thank you for choosing Auto Auto."

Stepping from the car, Cruz arched his back and heard his spine crack. Above him, streamers of gauzy white clouds were muting the blue sky. The warm breeze feathered his hair, and he caught a whiff of meat cooking. The lodge was a one-story redbrick building with a thatch-covered roof. Peacocks roamed freely around a manicured lawn with a kidney-shaped flagstone wading pond. Nearby, an arched trellis with a tangle of vines led to a porch lined with wood rocking chairs, their paint peeling like potato skins.

Aunt Marisol was rushing through the arbor toward them. "You made it."

"Finally." Dr. Vanderwick strolled to the back of the car. Team Cousteau followed to begin unloading their baggage and gear.

"Explorers, get settled in your rooms and then head out to the deck and get something to eat," instructed Aunt Marisol. "It's delicious— grilled meat skewers called sosaties, baked bread, and carrot-and-bean salad."

"I'm starving," said Emmett.

Lani slapped a hand to her head. "Unbelievable."

"Pygmy shrew, I'm tellin' ya," muttered Sailor, lifting her duffel out of the trunk.

When Cruz reached for the case marked *EA Tech Lab—Orion*, Dr. Vanderwick put a hand on his arm. "You can leave the SHOT-bot gear, Cruz. I'm going over to the research center to get everything ready for deployment."

"You mean, now?" choked Cruz. "You're going now?"

"Yes. I always feel better when I know everything is organized and ready to go."

"Can I go? I . . . uh . . . You know, to help you."

Dr. Vanderwick took a sip of water from her bottle. "Don't you want to get lunch?"

"I'm not hungry," he lied. "I'd really like to go see the conservation center."

"Yes, you can come, as long as your aunt doesn't have anything planned."

"It's fine," said Aunt Marisol with a secret wink to Cruz. "Give us a sec, will you? I need to talk to Dr. Vanderwick."

As soon as Cruz opened the right front door of their vehicle, Lani was at his side. "Do you want me to come?" she whispered.

"I should probably go alone."

"I'll take your bag in for you." She stepped back. Cruz got into the self-driving car. Lani didn't pick up their stuff and head inside the lodge. Instead, she tapped her chin with her index finger and sucked air between the little space in her front teeth. It made a squeaking sound. Cruz called it her chattering mouse mode, and it meant his best friend was more than thinking—she was *deep* in thought.

"You're not telling me something," said Lani. "What's going on?"

How *did* she do that? Knowing Lani, she'd invented a device to tap into his brain waves and listen to his thoughts. Cruz was still debating whether to tell her about Nebula planting a spy among the explorers. It would be nice to reveal this to someone he trusted, but it could also put her in danger.

Waiting for his answer, she'd added a toe tap to her stance.

Cruz leaned out the window. "Did you ever think that maybe the less you know the better?"

"Nope," she shot back so fast, she clipped the end of his sentence. "Usually, the less I know, the more trouble you're in."

He opened his mouth but couldn't think of one thing to say. Lani seemed delighted that she had rendered him speechless.

Dr. Vanderwick slid in beside him. "All set?"

"Definitely," answered Cruz, giving Lani a wave.

Mouthing "Good luck," she lifted her hand in return. Driving away,

Cruz kept an eye on her in the side-view mirror. Lani didn't move. Just kept standing there—her finger on her chin. He'd bet his dessert for a week she was mouse-chattering again. Cruz watched until the dust cloud obscured her. He tipped his neck back, letting his skull sink into the headrest. It wasn't going to be easy, dealing with a mind-reading, deep-thinking, mouse-chattering best friend. Lani Kealoha was, is, and most likely always would be a challenge.

Thank goodness.

WAITING WITH DR. VANDERWICK IN THE LOBBY of the conservation center, Cruz studied a row of framed wildlife photographs on the wall. He strolled past a flock of cotton-candy-pink flamingos balancing on one leg, their long necks and heads tucked into their feathers as they settled beneath a rosy sunset. Next came a photo of a mother cheetah and her fuzzy-headed cub. Illuminated by the golden glow of either dawn or dusk, the pair was walking away from the camera. As they headed down a sandy trail, the mother cheetah held her spotted neck high, her ears alert. The cub was reaching out a paw to playfully swat his mother's curling tail. Mama cheetah's footprints went in a straight line. Her cub's prints, however, were a zigzag of curiosity. The last photo in the row was a close-up of what looked like a miniature deer. Two short, straight black horns grew between a pair of long ears. From beneath thick curls of black lashes, big brown eyes seemed to fill its long face as it looked right into the camera.

"It's a Damara dik-dik," said a voice behind Cruz. He spun to see a tall, dark-skinned woman with close-cropped hair. She wore jeans and a white cotton shirt with the sleeves rolled up. "It's the smallest of the antelopes, barely fifteen inches tall. I took the photo not far from here."

"Are these yours?"

"Most, yes." Dark eyes with golden glitter on their lids crinkled. "You must be Cruz. Your aunt told me you'd be coming."

"Are you Dr. Jojozi?"

"Call me Dr. Jo." She tipped her head. "You look like her, you know."

"My aunt?"

"Your mom."

Cruz smiled.

Dr. Jo backed toward the hall, gesturing for Cruz and Dr. Vanderwick to follow. "I'll take you on back."

Leading them to the lab, Dr. Jo introduced them to Dr. Amuntenya, one of the other conservationists, who would be coordinating the explorers' mission. Even though Dr. Jo had to be close to six feet tall, Dr. Amuntenya towered above her by a good four inches.

Dr. Vanderwick unpacked the gear and gave a short SHOT-bot demo similar to the one she had given the explorers. "We can program the robot to resemble any type of vegetation," she explained. "We'll want to choose a plant that's compact, sturdy, evergreen, and that animals will avoid. Maybe something with thorns or spines."

"Perhaps a hardy succulent, like an aloe," suggested Dr. Amuntenya. "Ah, wait! I know! A truncate living stone. It has all the features we want and its leaves look like rocks, which will keep thirsty animals away."

"Cool!" cried Cruz. "A robot that mimics a plant that mimics a rock!"

They laughed.

"Let's find a good 3D image of the plant," said Dr. Vanderwick.

Dr. Amuntenya hunched over his computer. "I'll look it up under its Latin name, *Lithops pseudotruncatella* ..."

Within seconds, he'd pulled up a gallery of photos. Sure enough, the plant *did* look like a round rock a few inches in diameter that had been split down the middle. In some of the photos, a bright yellow flower with long thin petals was blooming between the smooth gray halves.

"I'll plug it into the software for 3D analysis and replication," said Dr. Vanderwick.

"Can we program each SHOT-bot to mimic a cluster of them?" asked Dr. Amuntenya.

"Absolutely. Once we get a complete image we're happy with, I'll show you how…"

Cruz felt a tap on his shoulder. Dr. Jo crooked her finger at him.

This was it! Dr. Jo was going to give him the fourth piece of the cipher! Cruz took a few deep breaths, trying to stay calm as he strolled beside her down the hall.

"Here we are." She gestured for him to go in first and shut the door behind them.

Her office was about the size of Cruz's bedroom back home. The walls were plastered with more wildlife photos of lions, wild dogs, elephants, rhinos, leopards, antelopes, vultures, warthogs, and some animals he couldn't identify, like a gray parrot-looking bird with red eyes and a chubby badger-like creature. There were so many pictures, in fact, Cruz could only tell the room was painted sage green by finding a sliver of wall near the window. Dr. Jo's office overlooked a small courtyard connecting the center's half dozen or so stucco buildings.

Taking a seat behind her desk, Dr. Jo caught him gazing around. "It's a hobby—okay, more like an addiction. Your mom liked photography, too."

"She did?"

"Oh yes. And she was quite good. She could have been a professional, if she'd wanted. The photo of the cheetahs in the lobby? She took that one—gave it to me as a gift. We'd trek out on a photo safari whenever we could while she was here working on her genetic diversity project."

"Genetic diversity?" Cruz had heard Professor Ishikawa use the term in biology class once, but they hadn't studied it so he wasn't exactly sure what it meant.

"It's the variation within the gene pool of a species," she explained. Cruz was still puzzled.

Dr. Jo went on to explain. "A population is healthiest when it has many different individuals contributing to it. When populations fall, whether due to climate change, habitat loss, poaching, or something else, it can lead to problems like birth defects and diseases. The greater the diversity, the better chance a species has for survival."

Cruz was curious. "What was my mom's project?"

"Her work involved cheetahs. These cats already have low genetic diversity, due to the mass extinction that occurred twelve thousand years ago. Your mom's genome research helped reveal what happened in the past so we could work to try to prevent further loss in the future. Her findings were—are—helping to save a species on the brink." Dr. Jo reached for an oval photo frame in the corner of her desk. "She was brilliant, your mom ... and yet, she never took herself too seriously. We had a lot of fun." She tilted the picture so Cruz could see it, too.

Cruz spotted his mother in the group photo. One tanned arm was hooked around Dr. Jo's neck. And his mom was grinning, almost laughing.

A weird feeling came over him—a mix of satisfaction and sadness. It was strange, but it was not new. Cruz had felt it before. First, in Norway when he was searching the seed vault for the second piece of the cipher, then again in Petra when he had discovered the third fragment in the Byzantine church. It was the realization that he was walking where she had walked, touching what she had touched. Cruz was fulfilling her destiny. That was the satisfaction part. The sadness came from meeting people like Nóri in Iceland and now Dr. Jo, who knew her and cared for her and missed her, as he did. It came from knowing that even if he succeeded in his quest to complete her formula, he was still chasing a ghost. She was gone. And nothing Cruz did would ever change that.

Dr. Jo was gazing at the photograph, lost in a memory. Her eyes were glassy.

Cruz's tablet chimed. The noise jarred them both.

It was a video call from Dr. Vanderwick. "I'm ready to head back to the lodge," she said.

"Uh ..." Cruz gave Dr. Jo a terrified look. He couldn't leave. Not yet. And they both knew why.

"Tell her I'm giving you a tour," whispered Dr. Jo. "We'll meet her in the lobby in ten minutes."

Cruz relayed the message then signed off.

Dr. Jo was unlocking her bottom drawer. "I have something for you, Cruz … It's from your mom."

Cruz drew in a sharp breath.

"I promised her I would keep this safe, that I would hold on to it for as long as it took for you to come and get it." He could hear the drawer slide open but, despite stretching his neck as far as it would go, couldn't see what she was reaching for. "I know this is going to sound a bit dramatic considering what it is, but I swore an oath to give it to you, and only you."

His pulse was racing. Cruz wiped two sweaty palms on the sides of his pants. Cupping his hands, he held them out across her desk. However, the item Dr. Jo placed in them was not the small triangular chunk of marble he'd expected.

Not even close.

19

▶ **"A T-SHIRT?"** Sailor wrinkled her nose. "Your mom left you a souvenir tee?"

Cruz was still in a daze, though he'd been back at the lodge for close to a half hour. He had been so certain Dr. Ziyanda Jojozi had the fourth piece of his mom's cipher. After all, the two had been close friends. And like his mom, Dr. Jo was a scientist. She would have understood and respected Petra Coronado's groundbreaking discovery. Yet, Cruz's mom had not entrusted her friend to protect the stone. Instead, she'd given her—

"Another clue," said Lani. The girls had hurried to Emmett and Cruz's room the moment they'd heard Cruz was back. "Let's see." Lani gently pried the white shirt from Cruz's balled-up hands. She held it up for Sailor and Emmett to look at, too.

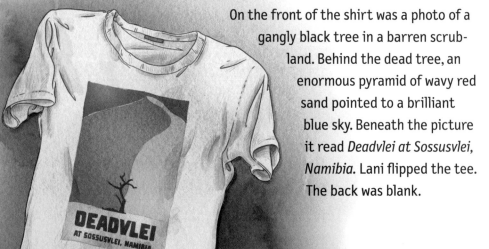

On the front of the shirt was a photo of a gangly black tree in a barren scrubland. Behind the dead tree, an enormous pyramid of wavy red sand pointed to a brilliant blue sky. Beneath the picture it read *Deadvlei at Sossusvlei, Namibia.* Lani flipped the tee. The back was blank.

DEADVLEI
AT SOSSUSVLEI, NAMIBIA

Sailor cocked her head. "Where's Sossa ... Sossu ...?"

"SOSS-us-vlay," said Cruz. "It's a huge salt and clay pan in the Namib Desert that floods, like, every ten years or so. It's got some of the biggest sand dunes in the world—up to a thousand feet high."

Lani traced along the wavy ridge of the pyramid. "I've never seen dunes this color. Or shape."

"Dr. Jo says they're called star dunes," explained Cruz. "The winds in the Namib blow from all directions and form dunes that are shaped like stars. Deadvlei is part of Sossusvlei, but sand has blocked the river's flow to it, so it doesn't flood anymore. Dr. Jo says the black tree in the photo is a camel thorn that died centuries ago. The air in the desert is too dry for it to decompose, so it sits there—a skeleton."

"Skeleton trees and star dunes," said Lani. "It's like an alien planet."

"Cool," said Sailor. "So, when do we go?"

"Tomorrow, I hope," answered Cruz. He was on his way to see Aunt Marisol in a few minutes to get permission. Cruz shifted. "The thing is ... with our mission, I have a feeling my aunt probably won't let *all* of us make the trip."

For a moment, no one spoke.

"That's okay," said Lani. "I don't need to go. I mean, I *want* to, but if you have to leave someone out, I'll stay behind ..."

"Same here," said Sailor, looking glum.

"Nobody will be mad if you can only take one or two of us," said Emmett. "Bummed. But not mad."

Cruz was relieved. "Thanks, guys."

Taking the shirt Lani held out to him, Cruz tucked it into the front of his uniform and headed down the hall to Aunt Marisol's room.

"Well?" she asked two seconds after closing the door behind him.

Cruz told her what had happened at the conservation center and pulled out the souvenir shirt as proof.

She shook out the tee, the charms on her bracelet jingling. "After touching base with Dr. Jo, I was so sure ..."

"Me too," said Cruz. "But I'm not discouraged."

"Good."

"I thought I'd go tomorrow."

His aunt draped the tee over a chair. "To Sossusvlei?"

Was this a trick question? She could see for herself that it was the next clue. He had to go. "Uh ... yeah."

"Cruz, the Namib isn't exactly right around the corner," said Aunt Marisol.

"I know, but—"

"You're going to travel hundreds of miles to the middle of the desert so you can search sand dunes hundreds of feet high to find a piece of marble the size of a ... a ... walnut? It would be like looking for a needle in a haystack—a harsh and unforgiving haystack, I might add. Are you aware that daytime temperatures in the Namib Desert can top one hundred degrees?"

"I've gotten A's on most of Monsieur Legrand's outdoor survival training programs," he argued.

"Maybe Monsieur Legrand might approve, but Dr. Hightower wouldn't." She paced toward the window, her hands on her hips. "And your dad—I can only imagine what he'd say."

Cruz sighed. "I don't see what the big deal is. You guys let me go to Petra."

She whirled to face him. "And you were nearly buried in a rock slide. I wasn't thrilled about letting you go to Petra, but it was a historic site with plenty of security and tourists. Not a hot, vast desert with snakes and scorpions. You also had Emmett and Sailor with you."

"I can take them with me this time, too—"

"Have you forgotten they have an important mission? So do you. We're deploying half of the SHOT-bots tomorrow and the other half the day after that."

"It's only for one day."

"That's *half* the mission."

Cruz felt warm. Prickly. Frustrated. "Aunt Marisol, you have to let me go!"

"Shhh!" His aunt pointed to the wall to remind him someone could be listening. "There's no need to rush into anything. Whatever is there will still be there in a few days, when our mission is complete. Let's calm down and take some time to think it through—"

"After the mission, will you let me go then?"

"Maybe...Cruz...I...I don't know."

Cruz had an idea. "You could come with me."

"I'd like to, but..." Her ponytail swayed. "I have responsibilities. I can't up and leave in the middle of an expedition. I am in charge of making sure the explorers get safely to and from *Orion*—"

Cruz groaned. "So, you won't let me go on my own, but you won't come."

He quickly realized he might have pushed things too far. She'd clenched her jaw. "This is exactly what I feared would happen—"

"What?"

"That your search for the stone would interfere with your studies," said his aunt. "I want to support you, of course, but you're an explorer, and that comes first."

"I know."

"Do you? I'm beginning to wonder. Cruz, this quest for the formula is taking up more and more of your time. It's pulling you away from the Academy, and I don't want to see you sacrifice your future for ... for ..."

He swallowed hard. "Nothing?"

"That wasn't what I was going to say." She crossed the room to him. "I meant the unknown. There's so much about the formula we don't know and may never know. Even if it turns out to be the greatest medical advancement in the history of humanity, it's not *your* achievement. Explorer Academy is about following your own path. Don't you see that? I admire you for what you're doing, but it shouldn't come at the expense of *your* dreams."

"It won't, Aunt Marisol," vowed Cruz. But even as he put his arms around her, there was a part of him that wondered if it already had.

Before dinner, Cruz decided to put the souvenir tee on under his uniform. As he was taking off his Academy shirt, he also accidentally pulled off the bandage on his ribs. Ali's scratches were now three pink lines. Guess the wound wasn't as bad as it had felt at the time. The shirt was a little big on him, but Cruz didn't care.

At six o'clock, Cruz and Emmett joined the other explorers, Aunt Marisol, and Dr. Vanderwick on the back deck of the lodge for a traditional Namibian potjieko. Chunks of meat, carrot, pumpkin, and potato had been placed in a three-legged cast-iron pot called a potjie and cooked for several hours over a fire. Spiced with onions, mild curry, and the orange-ginger flavor of turmeric, the stew was served with rice. It was delicious. Cruz felt better with food in his stomach.

Once they'd eaten, everyone gathered around the firepit. The last remnants of the sun were tinting the fringes of the horizon a fiery orange. Even with a full moon gliding up into a sapphire sky, the stars were beginning to glitter. The explorers ate raspberry-chocolate ice cream as they listened to a couple of the lodge's musicians play guitars and sing. As a courtesy to the performers, the explorers turned off their language translators. Cruz couldn't understand the Oshiwambo lyrics, but he liked the upbeat songs.

Finishing his ice cream, Cruz slid the zipper of his jacket down a few inches so he could see a bit of the red dune on the tee. Why had his mom given him a shirt without more specific instructions? It was sort of like saying "Search the Atlantic Ocean," or "Check the Grand Canyon." On the other hand, what if that was the whole point? Maybe he wasn't meant to understand everything. Maybe some things he was supposed to take on faith and simply...

Do.

What if this *was* his destiny?

Cruz's breath came faster as he realized what he was considering. It was a big risk. He'd miss one day of the mission. He'd be in hot water with Aunt Marisol, his dad, and Dr. Hightower, for sure. He might not find anything. Of course, if he *did* discover something, they couldn't stay mad for long, right?

If Cruz drove through the night, he could reach Sossusvlei by sunrise and, if luck was on his side, be back by this time tomorrow. He'd have to go alone. He could not ask his friends to get involved in something that could get them suspended. Or worse. He wouldn't tell them he was going. That way they could honestly say they had no idea what he was up to. Once Cruz was a hundred miles away, he would text Aunt Marisol and confess everything. She would be angry, but that couldn't be helped. She would forgive him.

The song was ending. Applause filled the cool night air. Cruz was ready to put his plan in motion. A server was coming around to dish out seconds of ice cream. Cruz rarely turned down his favorite dessert, but tonight he would have to.

He had somewhere to be.

CRUZ HAD NEVER STOLEN A CAR BEFORE. And technically, was it stealing? After all, the Auto Auto onboard computer had said the vehicle was theirs to use for the next three days, so he was merely taking the car up on its offer, right?

Cruz quietly opened the front-left door of the four-by-four vehicle. He looked to his left, then right. Seeing no one in the dark parking lot, he climbed in. Cruz set his pack on the seat beside him. Along with his water bottle in the side pocket, the pack held his tablet, safari hat, and some hastily grabbed snacks from the refreshment table in the lobby: an orange, a banana, a muffin, and a couple of small bags of cookies.

Cruz hesitated, his hand poised above the dashboard. Was he really going to do this? Once he tapped the power button on the console, there was no going back. His aunt was right. The Namib Desert *was* far away and conditions *were* extreme. It *was* a one in a trillion chance that he'd uncover a clue or piece of stone hidden somewhere among the monster star dunes. On the other hand, it was a place to start. He certainly wasn't going to find something by doing nothing.

Cruz took a deep breath, then pressed the screen.

"Welcome to Auto Auto, please input your—"

Cruz smashed the mute button. His eyes darted around the empty lot. When he was sure he hadn't given himself away, Cruz typed *Deadvlei, Sossusvlei* into the destination box.

Come on. Let's go, let's go!

Trouble. The computer was requesting biometric identification. It was a security feature he hadn't counted on. Cruz leaned down to let the beam scan his eyes. If it was programmed to respond only to Aunt Marisol or Dr. Vanderwick, he was done before he'd ever begun. It was a tense few seconds but, finally, the screen popped up with CONFIRMED. There was more to read from the computer:

Stops along the route will be made in accordance with charging require-ments and your preferences. Please let me know when you'd like to make a stop and your purpose for requesting it (food, rest break, etc.) and this vehicle will make every effort to accommodate you with a preselected loca-tion that meets our high standards. Enjoy your ride, and thank you for choosing Auto Auto.

"No, thank *you*," giggled Cruz, his seat belt clicking into place.

The engine roared to life. The headlights came on. The vehicle was backing out of its space. Cruz was really doing it!

Slumping down until his eyes were barely above the window, Cruz could see a swarm of miniature lights decorating the arbor. He half expected Aunt Marisol to come running down the path to stop him. She didn't.

Once the car turned onto the main road, Cruz straightened. There was nothing to do now but sit back and relax. It was going to be a long ride. He'd be far enough away when he texted his aunt in an hour or so that she couldn't come after him. He supposed she could call the police to stop him, if she really wanted to, but he was gambling she loved him enough not to get him in *that* much trouble with Dr. Hightower. A half hour later, as he was dozing, Cruz remembered he'd turned off the car's voice commands. There was no need to mute them now. He hit the icon marked VERBAL/TYPED COMMANDS, and asked, "Auto, how far is it to Sossusvlei?"

"I have no clue!" crowed a voice from behind him.

Cruz whirled around so fast he smacked his jaw on the seat. "Dugan!"

20

FLASHING A DEVILISH

grin, Dugan was lying across the back seat on his side, his head propped up on one hand.

"What are you doing here?" demanded Cruz.

"I could ask you the same thing."

"I asked first."

Dugan's smirk vanished. "I'd ... I'd rather not say."

"Same here," bit Cruz, facing forward.

This was a disaster! What was he supposed to do now? Cruz couldn't very well take Dugan with him to Sossusvlei, and he certainly couldn't turn around and go back to the lodge. Maybe he could drop Dugan somewhere? Cruz leaned forward, his eyes straining to see anything beyond the headlights. There was only darkness.

Cruz spun again. "Why didn't you tell me you were here when I first got in?"

"I ... I don't know. I thought you were going for a little joyride. Seemed like fun, but we've been driving for a while now and you don't seem very ... uh ... joyful."

"I'm not."

Dugan grunted. "So where is this sausage place?"

"Auto, how far is Sossusvlei?" Cruz knew she'd answered him the first time, but the shock of seeing Dugan had drowned her out.

"Sossusvlei, Namibia, is approximately three hundred ninety-eight miles from our current position," replied the female voice. "You will arrive at your destination in seven hours and thirty-seven minutes."

"*What?*" screeched Dugan. "No way can we go that far. Taryn will kill us. Your aunt for sure will kill *you*. We have to go back."

"We're not going back." Cruz reached into his pack for his tablet. "I'll text my aunt that you're with me and none of this was your idea."

"None of *what* was my idea?"

Cruz didn't answer.

"This is nuts," said Dugan. "Do you know that? You've gone completely pistachio!"

"I can let you out anytime," warned Cruz.

With a "humph," Dugan collapsed into his seat.

Cruz got busy composing his message:

> *Hi, Aunt Marisol,*
> *I'm sorry but I had to go to Sossusvlei.*
> *Mom's cipher is too important to me and*
> *it can't wait. Her dream IS my dream. Well, for*
> *now. I took the Auto Auto. But I promise to be*
> *very careful. Plus, I'm not alone. Dugan*
> *is with me. Don't blame him. He didn't*
> *necessarily know he was coming. We'll use*
> *caution and I'll tell you the whole story later.*
> *I hope you're not mad, but you probably are. I'll*
> *be back tomorrow night, and hopefully, with*
> *luck I'll have the cipher piece. That's a lot to hope*
> *(even if everything runs smoothly), I know.*
>
> *Your loving nephew,*
> *Cruz*

Next, he wrote to Emmett, Sailor, and Lani:

Hi, guys,
Don't freak out, but I'm on my way to find the
tree on the souvenir tee. I had to go. Dugan is
with me. I know, I know! He was hiding in the
car—I have no idea why—and I didn't find him
until we'd gone too far to turn back. We'll be
back tomorrow night. Have a good mission!
I'm sorry I can't be there. Wish me luck on my
mission.

Cruz

P.S. My aunt is going to be FURIOUS, so any-
thing nice you can say to her about me will
help. Guess I should be wishing YOU luck.

Cruz sent the messages, then shut down his tablet. He knew everyone would respond with concerns, questions, and, in Aunt Marisol's case, demands, but nothing was going to change his mind. Cruz had accomplished his goal: to let them know he was safe. There was no need for further discussion.

A quick check over his shoulder told him Dugan was settling in. His teammate was leaning against the car door, arms folded and eyes closed. Cruz knew he was going to have to give Dugan a good excuse for why they were traveling to the Namib Desert. Wriggling out of his jacket, Cruz balled it up and stuck it between the side of his head and the window. He didn't expect to get much rest, but the hum of the engine and the sway of the car were soothing. He could at least rest his eyes. He yawned.

"Hey, turn off the light."

"Huh?"

"That light," snapped Dugan. "It's kinda bright."

"I don't have a light on … except for the dash."

"Wanna bet?"

Cruz did see a faint glow.

"It's you," said Dugan. "It's coming from you. The back of your shirt is lit up."

Pulling at his tee, Cruz tried to peer behind him. "It is?"

"It looks like … words."

Cruz yanked the T-shirt over his head. Dugan was right! A message was scrawled on the back of the tee in glow-in-the-dark ink:

How is it possible to conceive
that the more you take
the more you leave?

"It sounds like a riddle," said Dugan.

"Yeah." Cruz touched the phrase he knew his mother had written.

"So what's the answer?"

"No idea."

"I bet we could figure it out." Dugan munched on his thumbnail. "What are some things you take?"

"Time?" offered Cruz.

"If you take your time doing something, you don't leave more time behind." Dugan bit his lip. "What else? You take advice. You take offense …"

"You take off in an airplane," said Cruz.

They brainstormed for several minutes, but nothing they came up with seemed to fit.

"Does the riddle have to do with why we're going to Sossusvlei?" pressed Dugan.

"Yes." Cruz flipped the tee to show Dugan the front. "This was my mom's shirt. She left it for me before she died … It's kind of … a birthday present."

Dugan held up a corner, squinting to see the photograph. He studied the picture of the skeleton tree and the star dunes. Cruz was already concocting a lie about how his mom had always talked about taking a family vacation to see the desert and that's why he *had* to go there.

"I get it," said Dugan.

That was it? No interrogation? No snarky remark?

Cruz put the shirt back on. "So you don't think I'm going pistachio after all?"

"I didn't say *that*. I am headed across Namibia in a stolen car in the middle of the night with a guy who wants to scope out a couple of sand dunes."

"Back home we have lithified dunes," said Cruz. "Ever seen dunes that have been turned to rock?"

"I live in New Mexico. I've seen tons of sand," puffed Dugan. "Ever been to White Sands National Monument? The sand isn't made of silica—it's gypsum. The crystals are clear, but their reflection makes them look white. They don't absorb heat from the sun, so you don't burn your toes walking on it, even when it's over a hundred degrees out. How 'bout that for sweet dunes?"

Cruz gave a smile of surrender. Didn't it figure that Dugan always had to do him one better?

They made good time. Dugan didn't need nearly as many stops or as much food as Emmett, and the charging issue that had plagued them on their first leg of the trip from Windhoek appeared to have been resolved. About halfway to Sossusvlei, the car's computer indicated it was time to recharge.

A few minutes after one o'clock in the morning, the four-by-four pulled into a station in Rehoboth, a city of 30,000 people about 55 miles south of the capital. No one else was hooked up at the row of charging ports, but several cars and a bunch of RVs were parked in the rest area not far away. While they waited for the car to juice, Dugan and Cruz stretched their legs. Cruz offered Dugan some water and food from his pack. Dugan took a quick swig of water and a bite of the banana. They headed over to the building in the rest area. The café inside was closed, but Cruz was able to refill his water bottle. Dugan checked out the vending machines while Cruz went to the bathroom.

When Cruz came out, he saw Dugan had bought a bag of red licorice. Back at the car, Cruz slid into his usual seat. This time Dugan got up front with him, and off they went. South of the Rehoboth city limits, the car turned right onto a well-worn gravel road.

Tearing open the bag of licorice, Dugan held it out to Cruz.

Cruz pulled out a long red twist. "Thanks."

Dugan chose one for himself. "I was talking to my little brother."

"Back at Rehoboth?"

"No, when you got in the car at the lodge. That's what I was doing in the back seat. I was talking to Rivik."

"Oh. Cool name."

"Cool kid. Most of the time." He tore off a hunk of licorice with his teeth. "He's being picked on, though, at school. By one guy, mostly."

"Sorry."

"Riv is kind of hyper. He gets excited about stuff like that, but I can calm him . . . usually. It's hard on him having me be away. I call when I can, but it's not the same."

Cruz understood. That's how he'd felt about Lani when they had been apart. "Is Rivik the reason you're thinking of going home?"

"I'm done thinking." Dugan's eyes wandered out the window to peer into the side mirror. "I've made up my mind. Once we get back to *Orion*, I'm telling Taryn I'm leaving."

Cruz dropped his licorice into his lap. "No, Dugan! You can't!"

"You wouldn't understand. You've got your dad and your aunt—people who care. Rivik and I, we don't. Things haven't been so easy. Our parents have . . . problems. We get shuffled between relatives a lot. I'm the only one Rivik can count on, and right now all he knows is I'm too far away to help."

"So, you'll talk more often," said Cruz. "Every day, if he wants. You don't have to leave the Academy."

"Thanks, but it's okay." Dugan sighed. "I'm not upset about it. I knew when I started the school year it might not work out."

"But we're not even halfway through—"

"He was crying, Cruz." Dugan's voice broke. "Tonight, Rivik was crying on the phone. That's why I came out to the car. I had to have some privacy so I could tell him about my decision. I can't let my brother down. Not after everyone else has. I have to go home."

Cruz dipped his head. It was hard to argue with Dugan. If his own father needed him, Cruz would leave the Academy in a second. Family came first.

"Hearing how Riv is getting pushed around," continued Dugan, "it also made me realize that some of the things I've said to you, things I thought were no big deal were a *big* deal. I . . . I shouldn't have given you a hard time about your aunt or how you got into the Academy. I was a real jerk."

"No permanent damage done," said Cruz. "But thanks."

"And for the record, I think Ali's wrong about you, too."

"He's still pretty steamed about Bwindi, huh?"

"He can be mad, but that's no reason for him to target you the way he did at the Talustrike match. Monsieur Legrand's view was blocked; otherwise he would have called a foul for sure."

Cruz nodded. He'd wondered why his instructor had let Ali's cheap shot pass.

"From now on, watch your back around Ali," cautioned Dugan. "He may be quiet, but he can hold a grudge."

"Okay."

"One other thing you might want to know." Dugan was glancing at his side mirror again.

"What's that?"

"We're being followed."

Cruz whipped around. A pair of headlights was behind them, though the vehicle seemed to be keeping a safe distance. The beams sat up high. They had to belong to a truck.

"How do you know they're following *us* and not just following us?"

"Because they stopped when we stopped at the charging station, then came out right behind us when we got back on the road," said Dugan. "Didn't you notice?"

Cruz had to admit he hadn't. He ought to have been paying more attention, given what he knew about Nebula.

"There's one way to know for sure," said Cruz. "I'll slow down a little. Let's see if they pass." The speedometer read 46 miles an hour. "Auto, please lower speed to forty miles an hour."

As they slowed, the truck behind them matched their speed.

Cruz dropped their speed another five miles. The truck did the same. Cruz didn't like this. He didn't like games. He also didn't want to lose time getting to Sossusvlei. He was about to up their vehicle's speed again, when the headlights behind them moved closer.

"They're going to go around," said Dugan.

Cruz let out a grateful breath. "Good."

The lights loomed closer ... and closer ...

Cruz stared at the rearview mirror, anticipating the blinking light that would indicate the truck was about to slide over into the right lane of the two-way gravel road. No one was coming from the other direction. "Anytime," he muttered.

The truck was now right up on their back bumper, the headlights blinding Cruz. If it didn't move over soon, it was going to—

Thump!

Cruz's neck snapped forward, his seat belt the only thing keeping him from being flung into the dash.

"Did you ...? They just ..." yelled Dugan.

"Yep." Cruz's heart was pounding. "Auto, increase—"

Bang!

This impact was harder.

"This vehicle has been involved in a minor collision," said the onboard computer. "As per Auto Auto regulations, your vehicle will now pull over so that you may exchange insurance information—"

"NO!" shouted Cruz and Dugan.

"Do not pull over," cried Dugan.

"Auto, increase speed! Increase speed!" ordered Cruz.

The four-by-four computer complied. They were accelerating, but so was the truck behind them. Cruz could only dig his fingernails into his seat and watch the speedometer rise.

38 . . . 42 . . . 46 . . . 50 . . .

They heard the car's gears shifting.

49 . . . 47 . . .

"No!" shrieked Dugan. "It's going down. Cruz, what are you doing?"

"Nothing. It's the computer—"

"Faster!" cried Dugan. "They're right up on our tail. Auto, we have to go faster!"

"I'm sorry," the computer said calmly. "The maximum speed limit on this road is fifty miles per hour. Auto Auto's state-of-the-art sensory system automatically analyzes road conditions and adjusts speeds accordingly. Rest assured, you are traveling at a safe speed—"

Suddenly, everything was a blur. Cruz saw white lights and red dust and Dugan's face and white lights and red rocks and Dugan's face. He heard nothing. It was all images, all spiraling out of control.

Cruz was spinning and spinning and spinning . . .

21

AS QUICKLY as it began, the tornado stopped.

Cruz was slumped forward, his shoulder jammed against the door. He lifted his head. Still dizzy and in the dark, he didn't know which direction the car was pointing or even where the road was, but at least they were right side up. The engine was still running, the headlights on. Looking out the windshield, Cruz gasped. Their four-by-four had spun to a halt less than five feet from the edge of a drop-off! Cruz couldn't be sure, but it looked like some kind of abandoned mining pit.

The truck that had caused their accident was nowhere in sight.

"On behalf of everyone at Auto Auto, we are terribly sorry you have been involved in a collision," said the computer. "Do any passengers require medical assistance?"

"Dugan," croaked Cruz.

His teammate moaned.

"Are you all right?" asked Cruz.

"I think so." Dugan slowly sat up, rubbing his neck. "Is my head still attached?"

Cruz checked him out as best he could. "You're in one piece. Auto, I think we're all okay."

"Our caring staff will be relieved to hear that," said the computer. "I am notifying our incident response team of your collision and current status. This vehicle has received minor structural damage but is functioning normally and is safe to operate. Would you like to continue on your present course to your preprogrammed destination?"

"Yes. Continue present course to preprogrammed destination." Cruz couldn't keep the quiver out of his voice.

"Enjoy your ride." The car made a gentle U-turn and found the road again.

This time, Cruz kept his eyes glued to his mirrors, going from the side view to the rearview and back again. No one was behind them. For now.

"That was wild ... and weird," said Dugan. "I thought they were gonna rob us or something, but guess not." He reached into the back seat. "Nothing like some idiot who thinks it's funny to go around frightening people."

"Joke's on them," said Cruz. "We don't scare easily."

"Right." Dugan's hands shook so much he could barely bring Cruz's water bottle to his lips.

Cruz knew this was no random attack. Somehow, Nebula had found out he was headed to Sossusvlei and had sent someone to stop him. Had Nebula been tipped off by the explorer spy? Only Sailor, Lani, Emmett, and Dugan knew where he was going. And Aunt Marisol, of course. Unless the spy had been listening in at the lodge ...

The boys rode in silence, watching their mirrors for any sign of headlights. Every now and then, one of them would swivel to check the back window, as if a reflection could not be trusted.

"You can sleep if you want," Cruz said to Dugan. "I'll stay up."

"Okay, thanks," said his teammate, but he did not close his eyes.

Cruz turned on his tablet. As he had predicted, everyone had responded to his messages. Emmett and Sailor both said they understood why he'd gone and to be careful. Lani's note contained two words: *Go, Cruz!!!* She always did have a thing for exclamation points. Cruz saved Aunt Marisol's note for last.

Dear Cruz,

I know how important it is to find the cipher, yet going to Sossusvlei when you don't know where to look or even what you are looking for is a fool's errand. It's also against school rules. Imagine what would happen if every explorer decided to go off on their own whenever they felt like it? Dr. Hightower has her limits. So do I. And you are testing them. We will talk when you return. Travel safely.

Love,
Aunt Marisol

It could have been worse. Still, he knew Aunt Marisol's use of the word "talk" was code for "lecture." He felt guilty for letting down his team and also sad that he was missing the first day of the mission. Cruz hoped Dr. Hightower wouldn't be too upset with him. As the year went on, it seemed less and less likely that he would follow in his mother's footsteps and win the North Star award. No matter what he did, he always seemed to be disappointing someone.

Cruz turned off his tablet to focus on the road. Occasionally, he let his eyes drop to the tiny blue car on the dashboard screen to watch it inch its way toward the green star that was their final destination. They still had a long way to go.

Cruz hoped they'd make it.

EVEN BEFORE HE WAS FULLY AWAKE, Cruz knew something was different. It took a minute for the haze of sleep to clear and for Cruz to realize what had changed. He wasn't hearing the car engine. Oh, great! They'd broken down. This was all he needed!

Reluctantly, Cruz opened his eyes to the first peachy rays of morning light. Beyond the front windshield rose the silhouette of red dunes.

Sossusvlei!

"We made it," cried Cruz, bouncing up. "We're here!"

"Yippee," said Dugan flatly. He yawned. "It's not like it's the Perilous Plunge of Panic roller coaster or anything."

Up ahead, a pair of gates was down. This is why they'd stopped. The park was still closed. Their four-by-four had pulled over to the side of the road until it opened. While they waited, the boys split the blueberry muffin and the orange Cruz had packed.

With food in him, Dugan seemed to perk up. He gazed at the dunes, then turned to Cruz. "I wonder if we find the tree on your shirt, if it'll give us the answer to the riddle."

"Maybe." Cruz popped a slice of orange into his mouth. He tapped his GPS pin, and the boys read the location description that appeared before them in holographic form.

Sossusvlei is where the dunes of the Namib Desert meet, blocking the flow of the Tsauchab River to the Atlantic Ocean. The word vlei *is Afrikaans for "marsh" and Sossusvlei means "dead-end marsh." Most seasons, the river never flows this far and the pan remains dry, but every decade or so heavy rains allow the Tsauchab to flood the pan. This temporary lake can hold water for up to one year. Sossusvlei is home to some of the tallest red dunes in the world, including dune Big Daddy (1,066 feet). This dune overlooks another interesting feature: Deadvlei, meaning "dead marsh." Like Sossusvlei, Deadvlei is a pan that also used to flood until encroaching sand dunes blocked the Tsauchab from reaching it. Now only the skeletons of 900-year-old camel thorn trees remain in the marsh, where the air is so dry the trees do not decompose.*

The car's engine was starting! The park gates were coming up. Flicking on the blinker, the car crept back out onto the asphalt to join the traffic heading into a large gravel parking lot.

"You have arrived at your destination," said the computer. "The current temperature is sixty-seven degrees. The weather is expected to be clear and hot today with a high of ninety-three degrees. We hope you have enjoyed your ride. This automobile will remain for your use for the next two days. Thank you for choosing Auto Auto."

Cruz hopped out of the car as soon as the wheels came to a stop. Beneath his feet, loose red sand swept across patches of caked white salt. Although they were surrounded by dunes, there was greenery, too, in the lowlands—trees, bushes, and scrub grasses. Even at this hour of the morning, the lot was beginning to fill. About to put on his safari hat, Cruz offered it to Dugan instead. He had come prepared for the desert conditions. Dugan had not.

"I can wear my rain hood," said Dugan, reaching around to unzip it from his collar.

Cruz put on his jacket and grabbed his pack, and they followed the other tourists in from the parking lot. Cruz kept an eye out for any suspicious people. There was a good chance that whoever tried to run them off the road was already here. Waiting.

The wooden sign at the edge of the parking area indicated the hike to Deadvlei was a half mile. Following the carved markers, the boys headed down the trail and across the scrublands toward the larger dunes. On their way, they spotted a huge plant with long, strap-like leaves and a cluster of cones that reminded Cruz of burnt dinner rolls. They figured with such wilted leaves it had to be dead, but their GPS told them otherwise. The system's plant guide identified it as *Welwitschia mirabilis*, explaining that it was native to the Namib Desert and that individual plants could live up to 1,500 years!

"*Welwitschia* would be a great model for a SHOT-bot," said Dugan. "Imagine those big floppy leaves following you around."

Cruz grinned. "Sorry we're missing the first day of the mission."

"We still have tomorrow."

As the boys walked toward the taller dunes, their shoes sank deeper into the red sand. The trail forked. An arrow pointing to the right read SOSSUSVLEI; the one to the left was marked DEADVLEI. Veering left, they trekked between a gap in the dunes and soon found themselves within the alien world on Cruz's shirt.

Dugan let out a soft whistle. "Deadvlei."

It was far stranger and spookier than Cruz had expected. And yet, there was a beauty to it, too. Skeleton trees dotted the vast oval marsh, their exposed roots baked into a flat bed of cracked white sand. Gnarled black limbs reached for the sky, even as their shadows clawed at the hard ground. But for the trail leading in, red dunes enclosed the entire marsh. The sharp angle of the rising sun highlighted the geometric shapes and bright colors of the stark landscape—white ground, black trees, red pyramids, blue sky.

There were only a hundred or so of the dead camel thorn trees in Deadvlei, but they were scattered far apart across the vast pan. Starting on the outer edge, the boys went from one skeleton tree to the next, comparing each to the one on Cruz's shirt.

"The branches on your tree sort of look like a ballet dancer leaping," noted Dugan. "Let's look for that."

They did their best, but 45 minutes later, the pair was hot, thirsty, and no closer to finding the dancing tree.

"It has to be here *somewhere*," said Cruz as they took turns drinking from his water bottle. "These trees don't decompose."

"Wait a sec," said Dugan. "What if instead of matching the tree, we matched the dune?" He wiggled a corner of his sunglasses.

Cruz saw what he was getting at. Dugan could use his GPS sunglasses to identify the dune on Cruz's shirt and match it to the real thing. With the shifting sands, the dunes might not perfectly correspond, but it would at least point them in the right direction. "Let's try," said Cruz.

Pointing his GPS sunglasses at Cruz's shirt, Dugan requested identification. "It says the dune on your shirt is Big Daddy." He did a slow circle, lining up the GPS guide in his sunglasses with the horizon. "This way." Dugan pointed and began pacing toward the gigantic red dune.

Cruz followed. "Hey, I just realized something. Since *vlei* is the Afrikaans word for 'marsh,' if you lived here you'd be Dugan Vlei."

Dugan chuckled, then stopped so quickly, Cruz ran into his ankles. "Sorry, I—"

Cruz froze. Directly in front of them towered a skeleton tree with a leaning trunk in the shape of a leaping ballerina. This was it. *The* tree!

With a quick glance around to be sure no one else was near, Cruz inspected the trunk. He ran his hands over the scorched, dry wood. It was so brittle he was afraid it might fall apart in his fingers. There was a knothole at the base of the trunk, barely big enough to stick two fingers inside. At first, he didn't feel anything, but stretching a little farther, he felt something, then ...

Click!

A hinge unlocked, and a piece of bark popped open, like a tiny door.

Cruz could see a folded pink paper was tucked inside the tree. His heart beginning to pound, he reached for it. He smoothed out the scrap on his knee. It was in the shape of a cat. Cruz knew this! It was a sticky note from the pad in his mother's box. Two paw prints had been drawn in ink on the paper. One print was slightly bigger than the other. There was no message on the front or back.

Paw prints? What could they mean?

"Uh...Cruz?" Dugan cleared his throat. "I think somebody's coming. Make that a couple of somebodies."

Cruz's neck snapped up. Two figures, wearing black head scarves, dark shirts, and jeans, were sprinting toward them.

"Let's get out of here." Cruz flung the little door shut and shoved the note into his pocket.

"Which way?" Dugan's head was ping-ponging.

"Up!"

He didn't need to repeat himself. Dugan took off, racing for the closest dune—Big Daddy. Cruz wasn't far behind. The boys did their best to scramble up a ridge, but running on a surface that was constantly shifting wasn't easy. For every three feet Cruz ran, he slid back one foot. Thirty feet up the ridge and he was out of breath. Ahead of him, a hunched-over Dugan was faring better.

"Hurry!" Dugan shot over his shoulder. "They're gaining."

"I'm trying..." said Cruz, feeling himself slip again.

"Lean forward," called Dugan. "Use your hands."

Cruz put his left hand in Dugan's left footprint, then his right hand in Dugan's right footprint. Climbing like a monkey did give him some stability, but still, he wasn't going fast enough. Their pursuers were quickly closing the distance.

Putting his palm in another shoe print, the realization struck Cruz: He knew the answer to the riddle on the shirt! It was obvious. He couldn't believe he hadn't—

Cruz felt a jerk. Someone had a hold of his pack. He tried to pull away but couldn't. He was stuck, pedaling in place. Cruz had no choice but to let the pack fall from his shoulder. He reached for the pocket that held his octopod. Suddenly, his feet were out from under him. He was on his stomach and being dragged backward. Cruz was choking on sand. He tried to spit it out, even as he struggled to break free of his captor.

"Tuck and roll," yelled Dugan.

"Huh?"

"ROLL!"

Cruz closed his fist around the sand. Flipping onto his right shoulder, Cruz closed his eyes and tossed the sand into the air. A man began to cough. Cruz felt his grip loosen. Twisting free, Cruz tucked his head and legs in and hurtled his body down the dune. He felt like a human beach ball, bouncing over the sand. He saw a blur of red and blue and heard a whooshing sound. Cruz had no idea how long it took him to tumble to the bottom. It felt like ages but was probably only a few minutes.

Once Cruz could tell sky from sand, he sprang to his feet. The men in black were charging down the dune on their feet. Being upright was slowing them down. Dugan was rolling to a stop about 20 feet away. Cruz ran to him, pulled him up, and they raced down the trail and across the scrublands. Tearing across the parking lot, the two explorers jumped in their vehicle.

"Auto, lock all doors ... Return to ... Egumbo Guest House, now!" huffed Cruz, lowering his head for biometric identification. "Please ... hurry."

"They're coming!" cried Dugan. "Go, go, go!"

The Auto Auto pulled out of the parking space and headed for the exit. Dugan and Cruz craned their necks to see where the men were—in a big truck, no doubt. But there were too many people. Too many cars. They lost track of their pursuers.

The four-by-four got onto the main road. A chain of three RVs trailed them out. *Yes!* Cruz knew the bigger vehicles would slow any traffic behind them. Even so, he wouldn't feel totally safe until they were back at the lodge in Waterberg.

"I was ... wrong." Dugan was still trying to catch his breath. "This was *way* better than the Perilous Plunge of Panic!"

"Are you kidding? That *was* the Plunge of Panic!" cried Cruz.

"Explorer Academy style," laughed Dugan. "We did it!"

Cruz tried to smile. They may have beaten Nebula, but Cruz had lost something very valuable in the battle: his pack. Inside was his tablet, and it contained something that could never be replaced.

Back when he was considering making a replica of the cipher to fool Nebula, Cruz had used one of Fanchon's PANDA (Portable Artifact Notation and Data Analyzer) units to analyze one of the stones. The PANDA had found traces of his mom's DNA, as well as identified an activity she was doing in the final days of her life. At the time, Cruz hadn't been ready to watch a new holographic projection of his mother. However, before erasing the results from the PANDA unit, he'd downloaded the data onto his tablet to watch when he *was* ready. Now it was too late. He would never be able to see it. It was his own fault. Cruz should have had the courage to watch it. He should have been brave enough.

"You okay?" Dugan was asking.

"Uh-huh," Cruz said. "I ... was ... uh ... thinking. I know the answer to the riddle."

"You do? What is it?"

"Footprints. The more you take, the more you leave behind."

"Duh! Of course!"

Cruz pulled the cat sticky note from his pocket. He studied the two paw prints drawn on the pink paper, one a bit smaller than the other, and thought about everything he had experienced in Namibia: meeting his mom's friend Dr. Jo, seeing her collection of wildlife photographs, traveling to Sossusvlei, discovering the note in the skeleton tree, solving the riddle.

Cruz grinned. Everything made sense now.

Watching the star dunes of Deadvlei grow smaller in the side-view mirror, Cruz had figured out something else. He knew, finally, where to find the next cipher.

22

TEARS POOLED in Dr. Jo's eyes. "I had no idea."

It was late.

Cruz was beat after the long ride back from Sossusvlei, but there was no time to waste. He'd dropped Dugan off at the guest house, picked up Aunt Marisol, and the pair had met Dr. Jo in the lobby of the empty conservation center. Certain that he could trust Dr. Jo, as his mother had, Cruz had told her about his mom's death and his mission to recover her serum formula. He'd also revealed why he'd had to get Dr. Jo out of bed to meet them here.

"If I'd known your mom's life was in danger when she came to visit all those years ago," said Dr. Jo, "maybe I could have done something ... helped in some way ..."

"You did help," said Cruz. "You kept the shirt. And you kept that." He gazed at the photo of the mother cheetah and her cub trotting away from the camera. Their paw prints were side by side in the dirt, the baby's tracks smaller than its mother's.

"I've always loved that photo," said Dr. Jo. "I told her so the last time she visited—the last time I ever saw her."

"She knew you would always treasure it," said Aunt Marisol. "No wonder she chose it as a hiding spot."

"If I'm right," added Cruz, getting a quick nod from his aunt.

They both knew there were no guarantees.

Dr. Jo carefully lifted the photo off the wall and turned it around. There was nothing on the back. The conservationist seemed disappointed, but Cruz knew his mother wouldn't have been so careless as to tape the stone to the back of the frame where someone might spot it or it could fall off. Dr. Jo quickly realized it, too. She led the way over to the waiting area, gently placing the frame, picture side down, on the coffee table. The three of them knelt around it.

"You do it, Cruz," urged Dr. Jo.

There were four tabs holding the thick cardboard backing in place—one on each side, tucked under the frame. Cruz slid the top cardboard tab to one side. He did the same with the other three tabs until he felt the cardboard separate from the frame. Holding his breath, he lifted the backing. Attached to the top-left corner of the photograph was a small aqua parchment envelope. Cruz peeled it away. He tore off the top. Pinching the side seams, he peered inside.

"Well?" pressed Aunt Marisol.

Cruz dipped his hand into the envelope and brought out a folded piece of aqua paper. He unfolded each of the four sides to reveal a small slice of shiny black marble— the fourth piece of the cipher!

"Hello there," said Dr. Jo. She leaned in to inspect the stone.

Aunt Marisol let out a ragged sigh. "Halfway home."

Dr. Jo looked at Cruz. "When you find all the pieces, what then?"

"Mom's journal said she would give me instructions after the final piece," explained Cruz. "I figure she must have someone she wants me to give the formula to—you know, a scientist who can finish her work." Dr. Jo dipped her head in agreement but Cruz saw a shadow cross her face. "What?" he pressed.

"A cell-regeneration formula in the wrong hands ... or even in the right hands, for that matter ... it's a powerful thing."

"I know," said Cruz. That's why he was going to do exactly as his mom said.

"Be careful about who you give the formula to, if you decide to give it to anyone at all," said Dr. Jo.

Cruz frowned. He had never considered doing anything other than what his mother's journal instructed. If he didn't give the full cipher to someone, what was he supposed to do with it? Keep it? Destroy it? Or did she mean ...?

Whoa! Dr. Jo couldn't be suggesting that Cruz perfect the formula himself, could she? He wouldn't know the first thing about—no.

He was a kid. *No.*

Cruz felt a surge of heat. Sweat began to bead on his forehead.

"If you ever need anything, don't hesitate to call," Dr. Jo was saying. "Day or night."

"Th-thank you," said Cruz, running a hand through his hair.

On the drive back to the lodge, his aunt was awfully quiet. If she was going to lecture him, punish him, or lower his grade, Cruz wished she'd get on with it.

He couldn't take this. "Aunt—"

"You aren't planning on any more trips across the desert, are you?"

"No."

"We will discuss your punishment when we get back to the ship, understand?"

"Yes."

"I have one last question for you, young man."

Cruz gulped. "Yes?"

"What in the world happened to the car?"

He let out a snort of a laugh.

His aunt couldn't hide her grin. She tried but couldn't.

By the time Cruz and Aunt Marisol returned to the guest lodge, it was nearly midnight. Emmett, Lani, and Sailor should have been asleep. They weren't, of course. The three of them had broken curfew and were waiting in Emmett and Cruz's room.

"Sweet as!" cooed Sailor when she saw the stone. "I don't know how you did it."

Cruz tipped his head. "You mean, put all the clues together?"

"No!" She rolled her eyes. "Spent seventeen hours in a car with Dugan Marsh!"

Cruz laughed. "It wasn't so bad."

Truth was, on the way back from Sossusvlei, he'd had some time to think about Dugan and Rivik's problem. Cruz had come up with an idea that might convince Dugan to stay in the Academy, but first, he'd need to clear it with Sailor, Emmett, Lani, and Bryndis.

"Bryndis!" Cruz swung to Emmett. "Any word from Fanchon or your mom?"

Emmett shook his head.

"Try not to worry." Lani touched Cruz's arm. "She'll be okay."

He knew she was trying to keep his spirits up, so he gave her a smile. Yet, inside, Cruz was anything but calm. His blood was beginning to simmer. First his mother. Then Nóri. If Bryndis didn't make it, that was three people who'd been the victims of Nebula's vengeance. Three lives lost.

And what about him? How many times had Cruz fought Nebula for his own life? The images strobed in his brain: fighting to breathe underwater in Hawaii, dodging plummeting boulders in Petra, tumbling into the well in Turkey, rolling down the dune in Sossusvlei. Cruz was tired of running from Nebula. Right now, though, he had no choice. He had to keep moving. Finding his mother's cipher depended on it.

But one day . . . one day . . .

Nebula would run from him.

23

"MY FEET ARE on fire," said Dugan, who was behind Cruz on the trail. "What good are thermic uniforms to keep your body cool if your toes are roasting?"

"I hear you," called Sailor, who was in front of Cruz. "When we get back to *Orion,* we need to have a talk with Fanchon about new shoes."

Cruz's feet were hot, too, but he was trying not to complain. Team Cousteau and Team Galileo, along with Aunt Marisol, Dr. Vanderwick, and Dr. Jo, had been hiking for more than an hour. First, they'd tackled the steep trail to the top of the Waterberg Plateau to release a trio of SHOT-bots. The view was worth the climb, even if the sun was barely peeking over the horizon.

Below them, the plains of the shrub savanna stretched out in every direction. The explorers spotted several different animals up on the plateau—a family of baboons on a rocky bluff, a couple of buffalo at a water hole, and a badger-like creature Cruz had never heard of before called a rock hyrax. Dr. Jo had said they were nicknamed dassies in Africa and were related to elephants! Now the explorers were navigating a rocky, thin path that wound around the side of the cliffs to reach a second, lower deployment location to release their last three plant robots.

No longer hearing Dugan on his heels or in his ears, Cruz glanced behind him. His teammate had stopped under a tree about 20 feet back and was drinking from his water bottle. Cruz stopped, too, took a swig from his own water bottle, and waited for Dugan to catch up. Replacing his bottle in the side pocket of his pack, Cruz saw that Dugan hadn't moved. Instead, he was facing the cliffs and squinting up.

"What's he doing, taking root?" Sailor was backtracking.

Lani and Emmett were returning, too.

"We cannot show up at the end of the trail minus a teammate," said Sailor. "Explorer Academy frowns on that sort of thing." Slipping past Cruz, she led the march back to the lagging member of Team Cousteau. "Okay, Marsh, break time's over—"

"Shh-shh!" Dugan tapped his ear and pointed up.

Cruz heard twigs snapping. And voices! Men's voices were coming from the ridge above them. His first thought was they were hikers, but Dr. Jo had said they were in a restricted area. Nobody was supposed to be here.

"Lost tourists?" whispered Lani.

"Maybe," said Dugan softly. "But at this time of the morning, probably not."

Cruz had a feeling Dugan was right. He looked up at the narrow trail that snaked through the rocks. It was a bit tricky, but he was sure they could make the climb.

"Oh, no you don't, Cruz Coronado!" hissed Sailor, reading his mind. "Have you forgotten what happened the last time we did this? I ended up jumping off a waterfall!"

"If they're hunting illegally, they're armed," said Emmett. "And if they're armed..." He shook his head.

"We can't ignore it," insisted Cruz.

"Oh, brother." Sailor puckered her lips. "This sounds familiar."

Lani stepped in. "What if we got a video?"

"It might not stop them," said Emmett, "but we'd have something to give the authorities *and* we wouldn't be putting any of us in danger."

Cruz dug his phone and MC camera out of his pack. "We'll be so quiet, they won't even know we're here."

"Where have I heard that before?" muttered Sailor. Looking at her teammates, she threw up her hands. "Okay, fine. But if we die ..."

Cruz messaged his aunt to tell her they were stopping for a quick rest break. She responded that they would meet them at the end of the trail near the lower west water hole and not to take too long.

Swinging his pack onto his back, Dugan took the lead up the tight, winding path. He moved quickly and lightly. The rest of the team fell in behind him. Cruz brought up the rear. When Dugan reached a ledge, he'd scamper up, pull himself over, and hold out a palm for Lani, who would then reach for Emmett, who helped Sailor, who gave Cruz her hand.

At the summit, the team crouched together in the thick brush. About 30 yards to their left, two men stood in the tall grasses, their backs to the explorers. Wearing safari hats and vests, they appeared to be setting up a snare. One of the men had a laser rifle slung over his shoulder.

"Definitely poachers," hissed Emmett. Thanks to the new magnification feature Emmett had added to his emoto-glasses, Cruz's roommate was the only one who didn't have to use his MC camera to zoom in.

"I'm trying to get a photo," said Sailor, "but they're facing the other direction."

"Let's wait," urged Lani. "Maybe they'll turn around."

They kept still, hoping the hunters would look their way.

"We'd better go," whispered Emmett after 10 minutes. "We'll report their location to Dr. Jo. That's the best we can do."

"Talk about frustrating," said Lani. "We're so close!"

"Hey, what about this?" Dugan had pulled the last SHOT-bot out of his pack.

Cruz and Emmett exchanged looks. Sending in the robotic plant to get close-up pictures of the poachers? It might work!

Everyone was nodding.

Dugan set the circular robot on the red clay and clicked the morph button on the remote. They watched the little robot sprout a cluster of stonelike leaves. Blooms appeared between the splits in the leaves, and seconds later, dozens of yellow petals burst open. Once the flowers had finished blossoming, Dugan hit the go button and away the little robot went—inch by inch. Dugan switched the remote to manual so he could use the dial to steer it.

"Not exactly gripping adventure, is it?" whispered Sailor, although she knew as well as they did that the bots were designed to move slowly so they wouldn't scare any animals.

All they had to do was let the bot get close enough to take a video, spin it around, bring it back, and get out of there!

"Wuh-oh," said Emmett, who was closely following the progress of the SHOT-bot.

Not seeing a problem, Cruz crept toward him. "What's wrong?"

"A pangolin is coming through the grass. She has a baby on her back."

"She's headed straight for the hunters," said Lani.

"Oh no!" gasped Sailor.

"That's why they're setting their snares up here." Cruz searched the grasses with his MC camera. "They must know this is a path that pangolins travel."

"Mama pangolin has stopped," said Emmett. "She's still hidden by the brush. If she stays put, the hunters might not see her."

Cruz's camera lens found the pair of pangolins. The mother was rooting around a tree. The baby was clinging to its mom's long, scaly tail. Eyes closed, the baby's chin rested gently on the upward curve of her back.

"The SHOT-bot got video," whispered Dugan. "But it's stuck in a ditch. I can't bring it back."

"Don't move, mama pangolin," murmured Emmett.

"Too late," said Lani. "She's been spotted."

She was right. The poachers had turned in the direction of the pangolin. The hunter with the laser rifle had taken it off his shoulder. He looked to be powering up the weapon.

"We've got to do something!" hissed Sailor.

Cruz zipped open the top pocket of his uniform. "Mell, on." She flashed her golden eyes at him.

"Cruz, you're not alone here," said Lani firmly.

"Right." Cruz turned to the team. "Ideas?"

It took less than a minute for the five of them to come up with a plan.

"Mell, fly to eye level, please," directed Cruz. The MAV zipped from his pocket and hovered next to him. "Attack mode. On my command, sting the two men in the safari hats due north of us."

She blinked her eyes twice to indicate she understood.

Dugan gave them a silent countdown. He held up three fingers, then two, then one ...

"Stage one. Go, Mell," ordered Cruz.

She was off!

Sailor, Lani, and Cruz got ready. They were next. Putting his hand in his pocket, Cruz brought out his octopod. He could see the hunter bring the weapon to his shoulder.

"Hurry, Mell," said Sailor under her breath. "Hurry."

Cruz's stomach churned. Mell wasn't going to make it. The hunter was lining up the animal in his scope. A finger wrapped itself around the trigger. Wincing, Cruz turned away. He couldn't watch the pangolins die.

"Youch!"

"Ow!"

Cruz spun back. The hunters were running in circles, wildly swatting at the air around them. Mell! She'd done it!

Meantime, mama pangolin and her baby were scurrying into the brush. The tree next to them was smoking. The laser rifle had missed!

"Second stage, go!" said Dugan.

Cruz took off toward the hunters with Sailor and Lani on his heels.

Mell was still stinging, zipping this way and that to strike her targets.

Cruz sprayed the hunters with his octopod. Both cried out, fell to their knees, and threw their hands over their eyes. The hunter with the weapon dropped it.

Sailor grabbed the laser rifle, Lani scooped up the SHOT-bot, and Cruz called for Mell to cease her attack. The loyal honeybee drone landed on Cruz's shoulder.

It was all over.

Emmett and Dugan were running toward them.

"We called Dr. Coronado," huffed Emmett. "The authorities are on their way. They want to know if we can safely hold the poachers."

Cruz glanced at his drone. "What do you think, Mell? Can we hold 'em?"

A pair of golden eyes flashed twice.

24

CRUZ PACED the rail along the second story of *Orion*'s library.

Sailor was peering over the balcony. "You did tell him to meet us here, didn't you?"

"At four o'clock."

"It's that now," said Emmett.

Cruz feared he was too late. If Dugan had already talked to Taryn...

Lani pointed. "Here he comes."

They watched Dugan bound into the library and promptly get a warning from Dr. Holland, head librarian, to slow down. He obeyed. Seeing them, Dugan took the steps two at a time. Once he'd joined them, Cruz motioned for everyone to follow him. He wove through the stacks to his favorite reading spot, a quiet corner between the travel books and the history section on the port side of the ship.

"So what's up?" Dugan studied them. "Why the secret meeting?"

"We have a proposal," said Cruz.

Dugan raised a suspicious eyebrow. "What kind of proposal?"

"I was telling the team about Rivik," said Cruz. "You know, about your little brother missing you. That's all. That your little brother misses you." He wanted to signal that he hadn't revealed that Rivik was dealing with a bully at school or that Dugan was planning on leaving the Academy. Those things were for Dugan to divulge, if and when he chose to.

"O-kay." Dugan gave a slow nod. Message received.

"Most of us have brothers and sisters," Sailor jumped in. "And being away—especially for so long—it can be tough on them. So we were thinking, what if we made Rivik an honorary explorer?"

Dugan scrunched up his nose. "Huh?"

"You know, like a junior member of Team Cousteau," explained Lani.

"We could make him a replica comm pin and shadow badge," added Emmett. "They'd have to be fake, of course, but they'd look like ours."

"Once a week or so, one of us could call him and tell him about our missions or hang out with him and talk about stuff," said Cruz. "We'd take turns."

"Maybe if he felt like he was part of the team he'd be less lonely for you," said Sailor.

Cruz raised his eyebrows. "So what do you think?"

"I . . . I . . ." Dugan shook his head. "You guys would do that for me? For Rivik?"

"Sure," said Lani. "If you think it would help."

"Yeah. Riv is gonna love this."

Patting Dugan on the back, Cruz said, "You're an important part of this team."

A grin warmed Dugan's face.

Message received.

"**FANCHON?**"

A forearm appeared from the middle of the cubicles, and a hand rotated. "Here, Cruz!"

Cruz navigated the tech lab's maze of walls until he spotted a blue head scarf with puffy cumulus clouds. Wearing an apple-green-and-magenta-striped apron, Fanchon was sitting in an empty cubicle. Well, almost empty. There was another stool beside hers.

"I heard Operation Animal Selfies went perfectly and you caught a couple of poachers to boot." Fanchon put up a hand for him to slap. "Nice work, explorer."

His palm met hers. "Thanks." Cruz looked around the sparse cubicle. "So what's up? Got a new invention to try out?"

"Have a seat." She sounded serious.

Was something wrong?

He eased himself down onto the stool.

Fanchon tucked a stray curl into the cloud scarf. "I ... uh ... Remember when you came in and borrowed a PANDA unit to study that fossil you'd found in Barcelona?"

Cruz stiffened. He'd had to lie to Fanchon in order to analyze his mom's cipher in secret. "Uh ... oh, yeah, right. Sure."

"Well ... I ... uh, accessed the PANDA unit after you were done."

"What?" squealed Cruz. "You couldn't have. I erased all the data from the marb—fossil." What was he saying? Of course, she could have. The brilliant mind of Fanchon Quills would know how to retrieve any data from any source.

Cruz couldn't meet her eyes. "And did you get a DNA projection?"

"Yes. I'm sorry, Cruz. It's only that you seemed nervous when you came in that day—"

Cruz rocketed off his stool. His mom's data wasn't lost, after all! "You have it, then?"

A cloud-covered head nodded.

Cruz could have hugged her! "I haven't seen it," he blurted. "I mean, I wanted to, I meant to, but I didn't ... I couldn't ... and then I lost my tablet at Sossusvlei."

Fanchon's eyes probed his. "Do you want to see it now?"

"Absolutely!"

Wait. She hadn't called him in here merely to apologize. Something else was going on. Cruz took a breath. "On second thought, I don't know. Do I?"

"I think you should," she said. "It's nothing disturbing, I promise." Given that the PANDA unit had the ability to project what a person was doing shortly before their death, that came as a relief.

"O-okay." He sat back down.

Fanchon activated the PANDA unit and set it on the table.

A half minute later, Cruz was staring up at a holo-video of his mother. She looked as she did in her journal, except she was wearing a lab coat and her long blond hair hung in a loose braid down her back. She was holding a notebook, her blue-gray eyes intently reading the handwriting on the page. Was it a journal? A logbook? The right side of the notebook was out of focus and much of the left page was blocked by her shoulder, so he could only read the middle.

> *cell regeneration has remarkable potential*
> *my hand when I handled*
> *it appears that Cruz is, too.*
> *the full power of the serum*
> *could change his entire life.*
> *I know I must find a way.*
> *How do you begin to tell your son*

Cruz swung to Fanchon. "I don't get it."

She was shaking her head. "I'm not sure I do, either."

"Is there a way to see more of the entry?"

"This was the best I could do, for now. I'm working on perfecting some high-def reconstructive software, which might bring a few more words into focus, but I can't promise anything."

"What about finding the original notebook?"

Fanchon grimaced. "I doubt it still exists."

"The fire," whispered Cruz, deflating.

"It might not be anything important," said Fanchon. "You know what it's like when you try to figure out the entire picture on a jigsaw puzzle based on one piece. It could be nothing."

If that was true, why did she look so worried? No, it was something, all right.

Fanchon's phone was chiming.

"Sorry. One second." She slipped the phone out of the front pocket of her striped apron. Cruz watched her read the screen, her brown eyes growing wider with each line. Holding the phone against her heart, she let out a tiny cry.

"Fanchon?"

"It's Dr. Hightower," she rasped. "She's at the hospital in Kampala."

Cruz felt the blood drain from his head. "Bryndis?"

Fanchon nodded.

Oh no. *No!*

Cruz backed up, crashing into the partition. It couldn't be true.

Fanchon turned the phone toward him. Cruz didn't want to see it. He didn't want to look. But he forced himself to. Cruz had to know.

Antidote working. Bryndis stable and recovering.
Thank you, thank you, thank you.
     R.H.

Throwing his arms around the tech lab chief, Cruz could only echo the Academy president's words. "Thank you, Fanchon, thank you, thank you, thank you."

Hugging her, Cruz's eyes were drawn upward to the sentence fragments still hovering in the air. What, he wondered, was the full power of the serum? And how would it change his life?

It was the last line that scared him most. Cruz stared at the frozen image of his mother and silently asked the question he knew she could never answer.

Mom, what secret did you want to tell me?

THE TRUTH BEHIND THE FICTION

Explorers and conservationists are dedicated to protecting the planet and all that's in it. That includes the amazing animals featured in this book—from the largest mountain gorilla to the smallest pangolin. Something these animals have in common? Their homes and lives are in danger, and they rely on the work of real-life National Geographic explorers to survive. Thanks to some high-tech inventions that help photograph and track animals, initiatives with local communities, incredible conservation stories written by journalists, and most of all the dedication of conservationists, there's still time to help. Check out these National Geographic explorers on the forefront of conservation.

JEN GUYTON

Professor Gabriel introduces Cruz and his fellow recruits to camera traps, useful devices that give researchers the ability to analyze animal behavior, species density, migration patterns, and, of course, get some incredible freeze-frames in the process! Ecologist and photographer Jen Guyton works for most of the year in Gorongosa National Park in Mozambique. She specializes in using camera traps to document wildlife in the area, and specifically studies how large herbivores interact with the plants they eat. Since camera traps can blend into their surroundings quite well, Guyton is able to

get some pretty rare shots of everything from hippos to vultures. Some of her best tips and tricks? Try placing the camera trap near a large source of water to get a wide variety of species in your shot, or near a carcass if you're trying to snap a scavenger.

VINCENT VAN DER MERWE

In the future world of Explorer Academy, cheetahs have been reduced to living only in the African country of Namibia. In reality, cheetahs are currently found in other countries, too, including Zimbabwe, Botswana, Kenya, Algeria, and Iran. However, their range is less than 10 percent of what it once was, and populations are on the decline. Fortunately, conservationists like Vincent van der Merwe are working to save this endangered big cat by researching genetics and pairing together potential mates in order to produce strong, healthy cubs. As coordinator of the Endangered Wildlife Trust's Cheetah Metapopulation Project, he has moved cheetahs to different reserves all over South Africa to hopefully reproduce—and it's working! South Africa is the only country in the world where cheetah numbers are on the rise. The process of moving cheetahs can be difficult, but van der Merwe knows it's all worth it: "The very best moment is when you get that phone call from the reserve manager saying, 'Vincent, we've got four new cubs that were born to the cheetah that you brought in here six months ago.' That is what really brings joy to my heart."

AUGUSTIN BASABOSE

Like Kalema-Zikusoka, biologist and conservationist Augustin Basabose believes that the involvement of local people is essential to keeping mountain gorillas out of harm's way.

A native of the Democratic Republic of the Congo, Basabose has been leading the conservation charge of great apes in his home country for more than 25 years. His NGO, Primate Expertise, seeks to create sustainable conservation in the Democratic Republic of the Congo through research, education, and community-based outreach programs. With only about 1,000 mountain gorillas remaining on Earth, the initiatives of Kalema-Zikusoka and Basabose have never been more necessary to keep these highly intelligent animals from going extinct. These two conservationists have figured out a way to keep the planet in balance: by giving power back to local people to learn to best manage the wildlife in their area. When it comes to any kind of conservation, addressing the concerns of human communities is just as important as, or even more important than, working directly with the animals themselves.

GLADYS KALEMA-ZIKUSOKA

After speedily answering questions about mountain gorillas in class, Bryndis earns the opportunity to go on a life-saving mission to administer an antiviral medication to mountain gorillas. The viral outbreaks that lead to deadly respiratory illnesses in gorillas happen in real life, and they're unfortunately passed to gorillas by humans. Luckily, wildlife veterinarian and conservationist Gladys Kalema-Zikusoka is taking a stand to help these critically endangered primates. She led a team that researched the first scabies outbreak in mountain gorillas and found that it traced back to locals living around Bwindi Impenetrable National Park. After linking the lack of health care in human communities to sicknesses in gorilla families, she created Conservation Through Public Health, a nonprofit that promotes not only better public health but also peaceful coexistence between people and the mountain gorillas of East Africa.

JANI ACTMAN

The work of conservationists in the field would do little good worldwide if nobody heard about their challenges and successes. Journalist Jani Actman, a former wildlife trade investigative reporter for Wildlife Watch, National Geographic's series on wildlife exploitation, brings powerful stories about conservation to magazine pages and laptop screens. Many of her articles delve into the dark world of animal poaching. Using the power of words, she educates the public about everything from the harmful

impacts of the exotic animal trade to the deadly effects of poaching animals for traditional Chinese medicine, including park rangers who lost their lives to save animals and their homes. She investigated the crimes of the illegal black-market trade of tarantulas, pangolins, and Asiatic black bears, to name only a few. But her work also sheds light on work being done to combat these issues, such as the use of parachuting dogs that are trained to help stop poachers!

EXPLORER ACADEMY

BOOK 5:
THE TIGER'S NEST

27.4920° N   I   89.3634° E

"**C**ruz?" asked the holo-video. "Are you okay?"

His jaw dropped. She'd never before asked him a question. "I . . . uh . . . uh . . ."

"Don't freak out," Emmett said quietly. "The program probably has a feature that analyzes your vital signs or appearance."

Cruz cleared his raw throat. "Uh . . . I'm all right, Mom."

Petra Coronado tugged on the end of her long blond ponytail, pulling it around to the front of her shoulder. "I'm sorry it was such a difficult challenge. I had to make absolutely sure that you and *only* you would enter the grotto beneath the minaret."

"I did. I made it in and out perfectly fine," said Cruz. He did a full spin to prove it.

His mom was looking past him at something only she could see. "I am rushing, I know, but I have to hurry if I am to finish these journal entries in time."

In time. The words sent a chill through Cruz. He'd never heard her acknowledge that Nebula was closing in.

Always before it was, *If you find this . . .*

If I'm gone . . .

Now she seemed to be saying, *when.*

When you find this . . .

When I'm gone.

It tore into him. His mother knew what was going to happen. She knew.

"... I may be asking too much," she was saying.

Lost in thought, Cruz had missed the first part of her sentence. Too much of what? Of him?

"I used to think that my regeneration formula was all that mattered, that to keep it safe no risk was too great." His mom folded her arms across herself, as if standing in a biting winter wind. "But I was wrong. I never should have involved you, Cruz, even by accident. Not then and not now." She lifted her chin. "I can't change the past, but I can shape the future."

Read a longer excerpt from *The Tiger's Nest* at exploreracademy.com.

ACKNOWLEDGMENTS

Encouragement is like air to a writer. Those who so gently and generously bolster us through the quiet struggles of creativity help us breathe. The people I am about to list are experts at this, plus each and every one of them fills my heart with joy. Thank you to my agent, Rosemary Stimola, whose wit keeps me smiling and whose wisdom keeps me on course. I am grateful to my stellar team at National Geographic: Becky Baines, Jennifer Rees, Jennifer Emmett, Eva Absher-Schantz, Scott Plumbe, Lisa Bosley, Gareth Moore, Ruth Chamblee, Caitlin Holbrook, Ann Day, Holly Saunders, Kelly Forsythe, Bill O'Donnell, Laurie Hembree, Emily Everhart, Marfé Delano, Karen Wadsworth, Tracey Mason Daniels, and everyone who has worked so hard bringing Explorer Academy to the world. Special thanks to National Geographic explorer Gemina Garland-Lewis, a phenomenal woman and book tour partner, who also aided in my gorilla research for this book. I am blessed to be part of a positive, energetic writing community like SCBWI Western Washington. Thank you, Lisa Owens, Suzanne Williams, Deb Lund, Janet Lee Carey, Dori Hillestad Butler, Dia Calhoun, Dana Sullivan, Laurie Thompson, Patrick Jennings, Dori Jones Yang, Martha Brockenbrough, and all my OAV writing pals. I am also lucky to be inspired by so many strong, beautiful women: Debbie Thoma, Amber Kizer, Bonnie Jackson, Sherry Bells, JoAnne Warner, and Karyn Choo. My heartfelt appreciation to Marie-Reine Cressatti and Noor Alibay, dear friends who also assisted me with their beautiful language. Finally, thanks to my parents and family, especially my husband, Bill. He is my breath. My life.